THE CRYSTAL ROSE

RITE WORLD 6: RITE OF THE WARLOCK

JULIANA HAYGERT

COPYRIGHT

This book is a work of fiction. Names, characters, places, and incidents either are products of the author's imagination or are used fictitiously. Any resemblance to actual persons, living or dead, events, or locales is entirely coincidental.

Copyright © 2020 by Juliana Haygert

All rights reserved. This book or any portion thereof may not be reproduced or used in any manner whatsoever without the express written permission of the publisher except for the use of brief quotations in a book review.

Manufactured in the United States of America.

First Edition March 2019

www.JulianaHaygert.com

Edited by H. Danielle Crabtree

Cover design by Moonchildljilja

Any trademark, service marks, product names, or names featured are the property of their respective owners, and are used only for reference. There is no implied endorsement if one of these terms is used.

❀ Created with Vellum

AUTHOR'S NOTE

I hope you enjoy reading *The Crystal Rose*!

Don't forget to sign up for my Newsletter to find out about new releases, cover reveals, giveaways, and more!

If you want to see exclusive teasers, help me decide on covers, read excerpts, talk about books, etc, join my reader group on Facebook: Juliana's Club!

RITE WORLD

Welcome to the RITE WORLD!

Free Novella:
The Vampire Hunt

Rite World:
The Vampire Heir (Book 1)
The Witch Queen (Book 2)
The Immortal Vow (Book 3)
The Warlock Lord (Book 4)
The Wolf Consort (Book 5)
The Crystal Rose (Book 6)
The Wolf Forsaken (Book 7)
The Fae Bound (Book 8)
The Blood Pact (Book 9)

Rite World: Blackthorn Hunters Academy
The Demons Kiss (Book 1)

THERE WAS A HUMAN SAYING I THOUGHT OF OFTEN THESE DAYS.

All good things end.

It had been a week since Keeran defeated his father and locked him inside the amulet. A week since Farrah and Keeran broke the spell holding Wyatt hostage. A week we had been pretending we were carefree and normal.

But we were far from normal.

The fight was far from over. We still had to defeat Isalia, her she-wolves, and Soren's warlocks. Only then, would we be free.

I lay back on a rock along the lake's shore and closed my eyes, enjoying the last of the sun's warmth. Fall was starting, and the air was already chilly after dark here in the north.

Somewhere in the lake, Keeran paddled, his legs and arms splashing against the water. A moment later, he went quiet. For some reason, he had been trying to sneak up on me lately, but how could he when I was able to hear his heartbeat and breathing from a mile away?

This time was no different. He submerged in the water

and swam close to the water's edge. With careful steps, he emerged and tiptoed closer to me.

"Don't even think about it," I warned, my eyes still closed.

"Damn it, you're no fun."

Dripping wet, Keeran threw himself over me. I gasped as the cold from the water sizzled against my warm body.

"What the—?"

His lips crashed over mine. Lost in the moment, I opened my mouth and let him in. His body pressed against mine as he teased me with his tongue, ripping a moan from my throat.

I wanted to tune everything out, to allow my mind and soul to completely melt into Keeran's arms, to make love to him right here, right now.

But there were a couple of problems. One, we were out in the open. Farrah or Wyatt could walk in on us at any second, and I wouldn't hear them until it was too late. Besides, if we weren't indoors and far away, Wyatt could hear us with his werewolf hearing. I just hoped that every time I had slept with Keeran, Wyatt had tuned out his super hearing.

Two, it was time to go.

After a week of resting, relaxing and pretending to be normal, it was time to face the world.

It was time to go to Unity.

Using my agility, I wrapped my legs around Keeran's waist and spun us around. Breaking the kiss, I straddled him.

Keeran reached up and ran a hand over the faint scars on my face, lines my arch-enemy left behind. I hated them. They were a testament to my weakness, to my failure. And, sadly, they made me feel self-conscious. I never minded the naked-ness that came with being a werewolf, but I did mind having scars permanently etched on my cheek. I turned my head away.

"Don't." Keeran hooked a finger under my chin and pulled my head back, but I avoided his gaze. "Don't hide from me. You're beautiful and nothing, not even these scars, will ever make you any less."

His words warmed my heart. Knowing he was being truthful, I returned my eyes to his. I shifted my weight over him, rubbing my hips against his. "Comfortable?"

"Mmm, oh, yes, I think I like this better," he said, a teasing note in his voice. It was great seeing him in a good mood this morning. Ever since imprisoning his father in the amulet, he had been quiet and snapping more at everyone.

I glanced at the silver and white amulet resting on his chest. His father was in there.

And just like that, my desire was gone. I couldn't touch Keeran with his father between us.

I shot to my feet. "It's time to go." He reached for me, but I stepped back. "It's almost mid-morning. Wyatt and Farrah are waiting for us."

Grumbling under his breath, Keeran unfolded his long, golden body and stood right in front of me, just a pair of swim shorts covering his toned frame. As usual, my eyes seemed glued to the muscles beneath his skin.

One corner of his lips curled up. "Are you sure you want to go?"

I rolled my eyes and forced myself to move. "It's not that I want to go, but we need to." After all, we had agreed to meet Wyatt and Farrah at my family's cabin at nine in the morning, so we could start our journey.

I walked away from the lake, and Keeran hurried his

steps. When he fell into step with me, he entwined his fingers with mine. "Can I at least hold my mate's hand?"

A smile broke out across my lips. "Always."

Walking side by side with Keeran like this sometimes felt as if we had been together for years. Decades.

Not days.

He made me feel comfortable, safe, loved—things I hadn't felt in so long.

As expected, Farrah was in front of my cabin. Her long, silver hair gleamed in the sunlight, such an odd contrast to the black leather clothes covering her lean body. A small backpack hung from shoulders, a sign she was ready.

But ...

"Where's Wyatt?" Keeran stole the question from me.

Farrah turned her bright, blue eyes to us. "Inside the house." She gestured to the cabin beside mine, where Wyatt had been buried for the past week. "He says it's better if he doesn't go."

By the moon, we had been through this already.

I still had to change and grab my bags. The later we left, the later we would arrive at Unity, and as it was, we would arrive late already.

"Go talk to him." Keeran let go of my hand. "I'll go change and get everything ready. Don't worry."

Would he change my clothes for me too? I let out a long sigh, trying to calm down before my temper rose.

I stepped into the small cabin and found the place neat, organized. Probably all Farrah's work since Wyatt barely moved. Once arriving, he had sat down on the frail couch in the living room and only gotten up a handful of times. His brown eyes stared ahead, at a blank spot on the plain wall.

Ready for the fight that was sure to come, I put my hands

on my waist. "Why aren't you ready?" He didn't answer. "Wyatt, by the moon, don't make me pull rank on you."

Slowly, Wyatt turned his gaze to me—a deep sadness etched into his eyes. "Because I shouldn't be with you."

A growl started low in my chest. We had already talked about this. More than once, actually.

A few weeks ago, Wyatt had been spelled by Soren, practically brainwashed. On Soren's orders, he had killed many innocent supernaturals—and he remembered it all. Farrah had told me he had many nightmares and often woke up screaming, drenched in a cold sweat.

Farrah, Keeran, and I had told him it wasn't his fault. He wasn't himself when he was acting that way. It wasn't his will. But it didn't matter. The images were carved in his mind, and now he had to relive them all while conscious of how wrong all of it had been.

I understood, but I also thought that if he allowed himself to fall into a deep depression, he would never be able to pull himself out of it.

Since he didn't seem to care, the rest of us were making choices for him, and our first decision was to take Wyatt with us to Unity. Hopefully, we would be able to relax and heal while we waited for Isalia to give birth.

All that mattered was that he was okay in the end.

"By the moon, Wyatt ..." I counted to ten, then twenty, before I lost my patience. "I'm sorry, but I'm going to pull rank. You are coming with us. Right now. That's an order."

His gaze hardened. A moment later, he stood from the couch. Being almost one head taller than me, he could have been truly fearsome, but with his depression and close-off behavior, I could only sympathize with him.

"As you wish," he said through gritted teeth.

"Get your things and meet us outside in ten minutes," I ordered. That should be enough time for me to change my clothes and get my bag.

Like an obedient pup, Wyatt lowered his head. "Ok."

A mix of anger,frustration and sympathy filled my chest and pushed past my ribs. I stomped out of the house, knowing Wyatt would follow through with my order.

Farrah stared at me with big eyes as I stomp past her. "So? Is he coming?"

I snorted. Did she have any doubt I wouldn't make him come? "Of course."

The young fae girl let out a long, relieved breath. She whispered some words in fae, then said, "Thank you."

I waved her off and walked into my house to get ready. We didn't have time to waste.

WE TRUDGED THROUGH THE FOREST, TOWARD THE HIDDEN town. Keeran marched by my side, while Farrah trailed a few steps behind us.

Wyatt, though, was yards away. I kept my ears trained on him, in case he decided to run. Oh, I wouldn't let him. Not because I wanted him to stay and be part of our two-wolf pack, but because I was worried about him. If he stayed alone now, I wasn't sure what he would do.

Being the only warlock in the group, Keeran didn't have the same stamina or endurance as Farrah, Wyatt, and me. He tried hiding it, but I could hear his fast heartbeat and labored breathing.

Judging that we had made good time so far, I slowed my pace. Hopefully, it would be enough to allow him to catch his breath before we arrived in Unity—which would be in less than an hour.

In the moonlit darkness, the four of us kept going, our senses alert, and our minds eager to get to this hidden paradise. To be honest, I was the one eager to show them how all supernaturals could coexist in harmony.

"Wait," Farrah said forty minutes later.

Keeran and I slowed down and let her fell into step with us. "What is it?" I asked.

"I can sense something." She glanced around, as if searching for something no one else could see.

I opened my wolf senses, hoping to find whatever she had felt, but other than the forest creatures, there was nothing. "I don't hear or feel anything."

"What is it?" Keeran asked.

Farrah pressed a hand to her chest. "It's odd. I can't really tell." She searched the area more.

Wyatt approached us, his posture tense, but his eyes were soft toward the young fae. "What is it?"

Farrah dropped her hand. "It's nothing. Let's keep going."

Without looking at Wyatt, Farrah walked on. Keeran and I followed her, but Wyatt waited, putting space between us and him again.

I wondered if there was a way I could help him, other than kick his ass. I wasn't good at this sort of thing, but I was starting to think that if I waited for him to come around, I would end up losing him.

We plodded on, this time with Farrah in front. I couldn't help but notice how she tensed and glanced around, as if she sensed whatever had spooked her.

Why couldn't I sense it, though? Was it just a fae thing? I

would have to ask her about it later, once she didn't look so edgy.

Eagerness laced my chest as I recognized the shape of the trees snaking up a hill. "We're close," I announced.

Without meaning to, I hurried my steps.

We went up the hill, then down the other side, and into a line of trees. To anyone else, it looked like random trees in the forest, but I knew where to look—when in the right spot, the trees flanked a narrow trail. I guided our group down the trail and—

I halted, sensing people a few seconds before they walked from behind the trees and bushes and surrounded us.

"What ...?" Keeran would probably have cursed, but his voice faded as a few orbs of white light flooded the darkness, showing us the group of soldiers pointing their spears at us.

Werewolves, vampires, witches, and even a fae.

Wyatt, who had been farther behind, was pushed toward us by two warlocks, their long, sharp spears pointed at his back.

"I think Unity isn't happy to see us," Wyatt whispered.

I raised my hands and looked around, trying to find a face I recognized among the soldiers. One of them was bound to remember me, right? "We're not looking for trouble."

The sea of soldiers parted and a tall woman wearing a white and gray dress walked past them, toward us.

Almae smiled at us. "Welcome to Unity."

2

KEERAN

I MET THE EYES OF THE WITCH STANDING A FEW FEET FROM US.

She was tall with brown eyes, long brown hair, and an easy smile. From her thin nose, high cheekbones, thick eyebrows, and the slightly squared chin, there was no doubt this woman was my mother.

I had searched for her for the last few weeks, eager to meet her, but now that she stood in front of me, my feelings turned sour.

"Keeran," she whispered. Her eyes filled with tears. "My dear Keeran." She pulled me into her arms and embraced me tight.

My mother's first hug, and I couldn't even bring myself to hug her back.

She pulled back and cupped my face. "You're even more handsome in person."

I frowned. Had she seen me somewhere before? I really hoped not, or my rapidly increasing anger toward her would turn into red-hot fury.

"Did you see us coming?" Luana asked.

Acalla smiled at my mate. "I did." She glanced to the rest of the group. "And you two must be Farrah and Wyatt. Welcome to Unity." With her hand still on my arm, she beckoned us forward. "Come, come. I've got dinner almost ready."

The guards dropped their weapons, and stood back as Acalla walked into Unity. The floating orb lights trailed alongside them. Luana slipped her hand into mine and tugged me with her. Farrah and Wyatt followed right behind us.

As we walked down the narrow path, the scene opened, and even though the orb faded away, I could see the roofs of the houses under the moonlight, and the many lamps dotting the valley at the base of the mountain.

Acalla pointed to places on our way. The square, the school, the marketplace, the infirmary, among other things. The buildings and houses were all simple, but well cared for. The path changed from stones to cement, depending on the path or street. There were flowerbeds and manicured bushes all around.

But the most shocking was seeing the supernatural races together. This late at night, there weren't many people out, but it was odd seeing them strolling and chatting and laughing as if they were normal humans, as if there weren't a powerful supernatural world outside, as if there weren't any wars being fought or groups that needed allies.

Meanwhile, they hid here, pretending none of that mattered.

That thought was like fuel thrown at the flames.

Eventually, Acalla guided us down a path that went up a short hill and into her house.

She opened the door and let us pass. "Please, come in."

Luana walked in without ceremony, but I hesitated. If it

weren't for Luana's hand still secured in mine, I would have stayed outside.

I didn't know what I was expecting. Acalla's house was a normal place, maybe a little too cozy and rustic for my taste, but the place had style, and the smell of beef stew and spices filled the air, making my stomach grumble.

Luana threw me a knowing smile. I pressed a hand over my stomach.

After the four of us piled in to her small living room, Acalla closed the door.

"Thank you for having us," Farrah said.

"Oh, it's my pleasure." Acalla glanced at me before turning toward the kitchen. "Please, make yourselves comfortable at the table. I'll bring out the food."

Luana pushed me toward the rectangular table—there were five places set with plates, utensils, and glasses. Acalla had really seen us coming.

"Sit down," Luana said. "I'll go help her."

Luana went to the kitchen with Acalla, and the two of them talked and smiled at each other as if they were best friends. I probably wouldn't have moved from my spot if Farrah hadn't nudged me.

Wyatt, Farrah, and I took random seats at the table. Not a minute later, Luana and Acalla came back with hot pots and set them in the center of the table. Luana took the chair beside me, and Acalla sat at the table's end.

"I'm so glad to have you all here," Acalla said.

"Aren't you mad at me for bringing them here?" Luana asked. "You did tell me about that prophecy ..."

Acalla shook her head. "The she-wolf is busy right now. We have time."

I forced my eyes to the food in the center of the table. Did she know everything about us? About our enemies? If so, how could she have stayed hidden, letting it all play out? Why didn't she use her knowledge to help us? Help everyone?

Too many feelings stirred in my chest.

Farrah inhaled deeply. "The food smells amazing."

Acalla pointed to the pans. "Oh, please, dig in."

Probably hearing my rapid heartbeat and tight breathing, Luana didn't push me. She simply picked up my plate and served me a little of everything—spicy beef stew, wild rice, and roasted vegetables.

It did smell amazing, but my anger kept growing, making me act like a teenager. While everyone stuffed their faces, I didn't even pick up my fork and knife.

"What's the matter, Keeran?" Acalla finally asked. "Do you not like it?" She pushed her chair back. "Tell me what you like and I'll cook it for you."

Luana reached for her. "It's okay, Almae. He just needs a moment."

Almae. That was the name she used here, not Acalla. Another testament that she had let go of the past completely, including me.

"Oh, okay." Acalla sagged against the chair, as if defeated. "Well, if you're craving something sweet, I made dessert too."

Was she trying to buy me right now? With food? Was she serious?

I shot up. "I'm not hungry."

Luana turned to me. "Please, Keeran—"

"It's okay, Luana," Acalla said, her voice low. "Let him go."

My fury spiked. "What the hell? Are you seriously telling my mate to let me go? Just like you did?"

Acalla's face paled. "Keeran."

I shook my head. "I don't know why I came here. To be honest, I don't know why I was looking so hard to find you. Now that I've found you, I don't know why I bothered to look for you. You abandoned your son to the hands of cruel witches while you've been living it up."

Eyes wide and full of fear, Acalla stood. "I didn't abandon you. I never abandoned you. I loved you more than life itself. I still do. Leaving you behind was the hardest thing I have ever done in my entire life." I snorted, not buying her words. "I only left you at the Silverblood estate, because I thought you would be better off hiding there than running with me. Soren had found me one too many times, and I had to fight him off. I can't imagine how it would have ended if I had you with me. All I can think about is that he would have killed you, or stolen you from me."

"How is that worse than being enslaved for most of my life?"

Tears brimmed in her eyes. "I honestly thought they wouldn't do that to you. When I lived there, I befriended many good witches who were good to the slaves. They treated them with respect."

I shook my head. "That was probably a million years ago, because the Silverblood witches have always abused their slaves."

"I'm so sorry, Keeran." The tears rolled down Acalla's cheeks. "I wish I could have seen that future. I wish I could go back in time and keep you with me. Soren would probably have killed us both, but at least you wouldn't have suffered as long as you did."

"I don't buy it," I snapped. "I won't ever buy it. A real parent shouldn't—wouldn't—abandon their children. But let's say I believe you. Let's say you were right and abandoning me was the best course of action, what's your freaking excuse for later?"

She wiped some of her tears from her face. "What do you mean?"

"As I grew older, as you founded Unity and created this hidden corner of the world, why didn't you come back for me?"

She shook her head. "Soren's forces were still out looking for me, looking for you. The moment I stepped out of Unity, he would have found and killed me."

Couldn't she have sent some of her people to get me? Couldn't she risk her life for her child?

The anger dissipated a little, giving way to exhaustion. If we kept going, I would yell at her for abandoning me, and she would ask for forgiveness. This argument would go nowhere.

I turned to Luana and only then noticed she had moved. She was on the other side of the living room, waiting, and Farrah and Wyatt were nowhere to be seen.

"Can we go now?" I asked her.

"I have a cabin ready for you," Acalla said, her voice hard.

"No, I don't mean that," I said, still looking at Luana. "I mean, leave Unity. It was a mistake coming here."

"Keeran—"

"We're staying, Keeran," Luana said. "I'm not leaving at this hour. At least for the night, we're staying."

I opened my mouth to argue, but I was too tired for more arguments right now. Besides, there was no point. Luana would nag me until I said yes.

I nodded. Without another word, I walked out of that cursed house. I halted in the middle of the street and looked up at the starry sky. A few clouds drifted, hiding the full moon from sight. I inhaled the chilly night air, hoping it would cool my anger and ease frustration.

A moment later, Luana stepped out, holding a set of keys in her hands. "This way."

WE FOUND WYATT AND FARRAH DOWN THE ROAD. LUANA TOOK us to our cabins—Acalla had given us two small adjacent cabins not far from her house.

Wyatt and Farrah disappeared inside their place, and Luana and I stepped inside our own. The cabin was a smaller version of Acalla's house, though with fewer decorations and warm scents.

Luana closed the front door with a loud thud and turned her hazel eyes to me. "Want to talk about it?"

I shrugged. "About what?"

She tilted her head. "Don't do that. Don't pretend I don't know what's going on with you, or I don't know why you're hurting, or that you are hurting." She took two steps closer. "Talk to me."

A long breath escaped my lungs and my head fell forward. Luana stepped into me. She snaked her arms around my waist and pulled me against her.

"I ... I think what upsets me the most right now is that she was living here all these freaking years, well and happy," I confessed. "She could have come for me long ago, and saved me from so much."

"She didn't know you were suffering," Luana said, her voice gentle. "She thought you would have found a good witch to help you." I did and the witch's name was Thea, but it had been too late. "I know that if she knew about your situation, she would have come for you."

Didn't she have visions of the future? She knew we were coming. She knew Farrah's and Wyatt's names. How come she didn't know what had happened to me?

The more I thought about it, the more the anger was replaced by sadness, by disappointment, and honestly, I didn't know which was worse.

"I don't want to talk about it anymore."

Still holding me, Luana pulled back and looked up. "And what do you want to talk about?"

I looked in her eyes. My mate's pretty eyes. Despite all the ugliness in my past, she stuck with me, she stood by me, she held my hand, and she had my back. Saying I loved her wasn't enough. She would never have an idea how much she meant to me.

But I could try to show her.

I brushed my lips on hers. "Why talk at all?"

"Keeran ..." Luana pulled back, but when I tugged her back to me, she didn't resist. I dove into her neck, and rained kisses up her throat. "By the moon," she whispered, throwing her head back, giving me more access to her delicious skin.

I licked her chin and bit down on her lower lip. She was so freaking sweet. Not being able to control myself anymore, I pressed my mouth to hers, kissing her hard and deep. Without breaking the kiss, I pushed her back until we hit the couch.

She let go of me as she pulled her shirt over her chest, revealing the black lace bra covering her full breasts, her tanned skin, and her toned muscles. I leaned over her and ran my lips over her stomach, up her chest, around the upper curve of her breasts, across her collarbone.

I pressed myself down on her, but Luana put her hands on my shoulders, stopping me.

"What's wrong?" I asked, startled. Had I hurt her?

Luana reached behind my neck and pulled the necklace over my head. "This." She placed the amulet on the coffee table by our side. "Now, it's all good." She tugged my shoulders down, making me fall over her. "Now, it's perfect."

A smile stretched across my lips. "It's only going to get better."

I sank into her, glad to be able to lose myself in her. Because I had never felt this happy and satisfied and complete in my life, and I couldn't think of anything better.

3

LUANA

Despite our great night, Keeran woke up in a bad mood. It quickly turned even worse when I informed him I had agreed to have breakfast with Almae this morning.

"She might have given birth to me, but she's not my mother," he snapped.

I stared at the damn amulet around his neck. If I could, I would rip that thing from his neck and destroy it, but I wasn't sure what the effects of that would be. Nevertheless, I wished it was gone. Ever since imprisoning his father inside that thing, Keeran had been irritable, snapping more frequently, in a general bad mood, and acting like a temperamental teenager. I sure hoped he learned how to control whatever was affecting him, or we would have problems.

Despite his protests, I walked out of our cabin and headed toward Almae's house. At first, Keeran didn't move and I thought he would skip it, but he caught up with me. He frowned and crossed his arms as I knocked on Almae's door.

With a big smile, Almae opened the door and ushered us in. "Right on time. I just finished preparing breakfast."

I greeted Almae with a hug, but Keeran only nodded at her, then took his place at the table. After helping Almae bring the food and drinks to the table, I sat down beside Keeran.

I took a small bite of a pecan pastry. "Mmm, this is delicious."

"Thank you." Almae glanced at her son. "Did you sleep well?"

"Fine," he said, his tone curt. With jerky movements, Keeran reached for the milk and coffee, and a bagel and cream cheese.

Almae's smile faltered.

Trying my best to be diplomatic, I asked Almae about the people I had met the last time I had been here. She told me about their daily lives, how the marketplace was still the most popular spot in town, and how the lake was becoming less crowded now that summer was gone.

I waited until we were done with breakfast—and Keeran had finally eaten something, since last night he had skipped dinner—to bring up the subject I was dying to ask about.

I picked up my plates and brought them to the sink, where Almae was washing them. "About the fight ..."

Almae shook her head, her long braid barely moving on her back. "I know what you're going to ask."

I arched an eyebrow. Why wasn't I surprised? "You won't help us, then?"

"I agree that Isalia must be taken down, but you know I can't expose Unity. Fighting that she-wolf would do just that."

I picked up a dish towel and took a clean plate from her. "I understand that, but what if you lend us a few soldiers. Isalia and the others will never know where they came from."

Almae's hand stilled. "It's too risky." With a sigh, she

glanced at me. "I only have a few fighters, and they aren't expertly trained. Besides, I've worked too hard to build this place. I won't let anything or anyone destroy it."

Behind us, Keeran snorted.

I ignored him and his attitude, but apparently, he didn't want to be ignored.

"Typical," he muttered.

Almae's shoulders sagged. She finished washing the plate in her hands, passed it to me, and then turned to face her son. "That's not fair. You might believe I was high and mighty all these years, but that wasn't the case. I too went through many hardships to get where I am now. I had to overcome too many obstacles to build this place, to keep it hidden."

Keeran's hands balled into fists. "So you're going to keep hiding inside your paradise while the world around you burns?"

"Although I won't get Unity involved, I did help create this mess," Almae said, her voice tight. From the rumble in her chest, I knew she was holding back tears. "So I'll help you clean it up."

"What do you mean?" I asked.

"You and your friends can stay here until Isalia gives birth to her pup," Almae said. "Meanwhile, I'll lend any services I can to your cause. If you want, I can teach you, Keeran, to be a stronger warlock."

"Who says—?"

"That sounds good," I said, cutting Keeran off before he said something he would regret later. "That sounds great, actually."

Keeran glared at me, but thankfully, he remained quiet. He only grumbled something about going for a walk, then marched out of the house.

"He hates me. He'll always hate me." A tear finally rolled down Almae's cheek. "I can't blame him. I would probably hate me too."

I walked to her and took her hands in mine. "Give him time. I'm sure he'll come around."

It seemed so odd. At first, Keeran had been so excited about finding his mother. Perhaps because he thought that it was an impossible task. Because he thought he wouldn't succeed. But once he realized she was alive and well, his mind started spinning and considering all that could have happened. Why had she abandoned him? Why had she never come back for him? Because of those unanswered questions, he resented her—and his resentment only grew with each new detail he learned about her.

If only I could do something to help them out, to bridge the gap between them.

The first thing that came to mind was to get rid of that damned amulet. That thing had certainly affected Keeran's mood. I bet that if he weren't wearing it, he would have received his mother with open arms. Of course, he would have wanted answers too, but he wouldn't have been rude to her face.

"I'm not so sure," Almae said. "From his point of view, I'm a terrible mother. Maybe I really am."

I couldn't understand the courage it must have taken, and the pain she must have endured, to leave her baby behind. I liked to think I would never do something like that, but I couldn't be certain. If I was running for my life, and put the baby's life at risk, then I would probably try to find a less dangerous place for him. In the end, none of the options were great, making it an impossible decision.

My heart hurt for them.

"No, you're not." I squeezed her hands. "Just ... be there for him now. The rest will fall into place."

She offered me a small smile. "When did you become so wise?"

I snorted. "Don't let a few pretty words fool you. I'm still pretty hot headed and crazy most of the time."

Almae let out a soft chuckle.

At least she could still smile.

Now, I had to figure out how to do the same for my mate.

4

I WANTED TO RESIST, BUT IT DIDN'T TAKE LONG FOR LUANA TO convince me to train with my mother. She made some good points, like the fact that my freaking magic was still unstable. Soon, we would be facing Isalia and her lackeys. While Luana challenged Isalia, Farrah, Wyatt, and I would be left to deal with the rest of the werewolves and warlocks. It wouldn't be a fair fight, and I needed to have more control over my magic, become stronger, better.

Besides, there was nothing else to do in this cursed place.

My other option was to leave, but Luana was adamant that it wasn't the best choice.

Because of that, I found myself dragging my feet to a clearing behind Acalla's house, where no one could be hurt if something went wrong. Apparently, there was a building on the main street where the few soldiers they had gathered and trained, but at this time of the day, a crowd of supernaturals milled around the place. I didn't want to hurt anyone, but I also didn't want others spying on me while I tried to get a handle on my magic.

Under the warm sun and surrounded by the scent of sweet flowers, Acalla was waiting for me in the clearing. When she saw me coming, her shoulders relaxed, and I could see the corners of her lips turning into a smile. But she reined it in and stared at me.

She clasped her hands together. "I'm glad you agreed to this."

Sentences like "who cares?" or "I didn't" or "let's just get this over with" rushed to my mouth, but I bit my tongue. If I snapped at her, we would argue, and I wouldn't get any training in.

I halted a few steps from her. "So, where do we start?"

Her eyes softened, as if she too had been expecting harsh words from me. "First, I want to see what you can do, then I can determine what to help you with."

We started with small spells—produce a bolt, cast a flame, put out the flame, juggle the bolt between hands, make it quickly appear and disappear, bring up a shield, reinforce it —then were moved to a little more advanced ones—throw the bolt at a target, make flames appear at a distance and control their direction, misdirect a bolt coming my way.

These were all things I had done dozen of times before during battle. Did I really have to pretend I was a kid learning to ride a bike?

Acalla threw a big white bolt at me. I threw my hands up and parted the bolt, but instead of letting the magic disperse to the sides, I grabbed them, holding them hostages in my palms. I closed my hands into fists and the bolts dissipated.

A soft smile adorned her lips. "That was very good."

Now, all I was missing was the freaking lollipop after class.

Irritation rolled through me in waves. I couldn't help but

throw more wood onto the fire. "I defeated my father, but didn't turn evil. Was that how your prophecy was supposed to turn out?" The smile fell from her lips. "What about the other prophecy about Isalia attacking here? That's why you want us gone, isn't it?"

Her face paled. "If I had my way, you and your friends would never leave."

"And yet, you'll kick us out when the time comes."

"You have to understand. As a leader, I have a duty to protect my people and—"

"That is not my problem!" Was she seriously saying that to me? Her people? Her people? I was her people and she hadn't protected me!

"Keeran—"

I took a step back. "It was a mistake coming here."

She swallowed hard. "To train or to Unity?"

"Both." I turned around and marched away.

I heard her long breath before her words. "I know you're not a true warlock lord yet," she said, her voice devoid of any emotion. I skidded to a stop. "You can take the title by force, but you'll never be the warlock lord, unless you kill your father."

I glanced at her over my shoulder. "He's too strong for me," I admitted, surprising myself. I hadn't meant to say anything. Yet, more words came out of my mouth. "I've tried, but I can't kill him." Acalla averted her eyes. What ...? I sucked in a sharp breath as a realization became clear. "You know something. Is there a way for me to become the warlock lord without killing him?"

Her eyes returned to mine. "There might be, but it's too risky. Besides, the problem right now isn't how to kill or defeat your father."

"What the hell are you talking about?"

She pointed to my neck. "I'm talking about the amulet you have under your shirt."

I pressed a hand to my shirt, feeling the amulet underneath. "Can you sense it?"

She nodded. "I can. I can also sense how strong it is, how it's stronger than you." She paused, pursing her lips. "I'm afraid to say that it's winning."

I curled my hands into fists. "It's not! I won't let it. I put my father in here; I can keep him in here."

"You won't. I'm sorry, but you won't be able to contain Soren's powers forever. Eventually, he'll break out, and when that happens, you'll have to fight him again."

I stared at her. "Was that a vision?"

"I don't need prophecies to see what is in front of me."

A growl started deep inside me. "You know nothing."

I turned and stomped away before she could say anything else. With each step I took, I felt the amulet pulsing harder, its magic calling to me.

It didn't matter what they said— Luana and Acalla —the amulet was helping me. It was making me stronger, more fearless, faster. I needed to be all that and more if we were to defeat Isalia and her army.

I needed the amulet and its magic.

5

LUANA

Since arriving in Unity almost a month ago, I had spent my mornings at the marketplace. At first, I talked to everyone and made more friends than my first time here. But over the last week, I had been turning the conversation toward the upcoming war. Almae said she wouldn't allow Unity to be directly involved in it, but she had given me the green light to talk to the other supernaturals and try to recruit them. She would allow them to join me—if they wanted to.

However, nobody wanted to.

They either had forgotten how unjust the world outside these walls were, or they didn't care. They were perfectly safe here, weren't they?

I wished I could get mad at them for that, but to be honest, I understood where they were coming from. Perhaps if I had lived in peace, I wouldn't consider joining a fight just because some strangers were in danger.

Despite knowing my name and a little of my history, I was still a stranger to them. Someone who had arrows targeted at her head. Someone who was destined to bring danger to Unity if I didn't leave soon.

Two months. That was how long we had before Isalia's pup was born, but I couldn't stay in Unity that long. To guarantee the safety of this place, my friends and I would have to leave a little before that.

And at this rate, we would leave without any allies.

By the moon, it was silly of me to think anyone would help.

I walked around the market, but by now, people already knew what I would say. After a couple more quick shutdowns, I gave up for the day.

Defeated, I dragged my feet away from the market.

My thoughts ran wild as I made my way up the hill toward my cabin. I thought about Keeran, who had been training with his mother almost every day since we arrived. He often complained about it and threatened to give up, but he always went back the next day. The prospect of having more control over his magic was too alluring.

However, his mood quickly deteriorated. He came back home every evening tense and upset. I wasn't sure if it was the amulet, or the sessions with his mother. Despite spending most of the day with Almae, Keeran still resented her. He snapped at her constantly, and when the opportunity presented itself, he was plain rude.

Which was so unlike him.

"There you are."

I glanced over my shoulder. Farrah ran up the hill and caught up with me.

"Hey," I said as she walked by my side.

"How is it going?"

I sighed. "Not good. No one wants to fight with us."

"I don't blame them."

"Me neither," I confessed. "But I still wish we could find allies. The four of us against Isalia and her army? That's suicide."

"I agree." She paused, but I could tell she had more to say. Farrah never shared much about her life, or initiated many conversations, and every time I tried to force it, she retreated. It was better to wait it out. Thankfully, this time she was feeling chattier than usual. "How's Keeran?"

"The same. He trains with his mother, is mean to her, comes back to the cabin, is rude to me. Rinse and repeat."

Farrah frowned. "Aren't you finding his rudeness a little odd?"

"I am."

"I think ... I think the amulet is influencing him. He might think he won't turn evil if he doesn't kill his father, but I think that's not true. I think that if he keeps wearing that damn amulet, all of its darkness will seep into him, making him evil."

I didn't want to admit it to myself, much less to someone else, but Farrah was right. That thought had crossed my mind hundreds of times. I was only deluding myself by ignoring it, wishing it would go away.

We couldn't pretend not to know what was wrong with Keeran.

"I don't know what to do, though," I muttered. "He has to wear the damn thing to keep his father locked inside. If he stops using it, his father will escape. And if he escapes, Keeran will have to kill him. Either way, he ends up turning evil."

Farrah nodded. "Soren is slowly turning his son mad

from the inside out. I think I would rather have them fight and get it over with."

"Keeran doesn't want that, not if we can't find a way to avoid him becoming evil afterward." Did he still care about that? Maybe the amulet had already corrupted so much of him, he didn't care about turning evil.

By the moon, I prayed he still cared.

"We can research that," Farrah suggested. "I'm sure Almae would be willing to help. Either with a way of destroying the amulet and Soren with it, or a way for Keeran to kill his father without becoming evil."

"I like that idea," I said as we halted in front of her cabin. She was holding a small red pouch in her hands. "What's that?"

"Some special herb mix Finch sells at the market," Farrah said. Finch was a grumpy warlock in his fifties with a knack for potions. Almae swore his teas worked like a charm. "It's supposed to relax you and bring clarity."

I knew exactly who this was for. I stared at the closed door behind her. "Wyatt."

"I don't know what else to do," she whispered. With his wolf hearing, Wyatt could hear her, even if she whispered. "Ever since we arrived, he spends the day locked inside this damn cabin, doing nothing. I tried dragging him to the forest so he could run a little, but he locked himself in his bedroom. I've already said everything I could think of, more than once or twice, but to no effect." Her blue eyes glittered with unshed tears. "I'm worried about him."

I was too. I had been inside their cabin a few times and tried to pull him out myself, but he only snapped at me, much like Keeran had been doing. Was Wyatt turning evil too? No, that wasn't it. From what Farrah told me, Wyatt barely slept because he was afraid. Every time he closed his eyes, he saw the faces of the innocent supernaturals he killed. Every time he fell asleep, he had nightmares. Those memories were driving him crazy.

My nostrils flared as I let out a long, determined breath. That was it. I would kick his ass back into gear even if I had to challenge him to a duel. If I won, he would have to do whatever I wanted him to do. If he won, then I would let him rot away in self-pity forever. I wouldn't even count on him for the upcoming fight against Isalia.

I marched inside their cabin. As expected, Wyatt was seated in an armchair in the living room, staring at the plain wall across the room. He was wearing loose sweatpants and a simple white shirt. His hair was a long mess, and his face was covered by a short beard.

By the moon, he looked terrible.

"Wyatt," I called him.

No answer.

Farrah dropped the red pouch on the side table and approached him. "Wyatt, Luana is here. She wants to talk to you."

No answer.

Farrah turned anguished eyes on me.

I marched right in front of him, grabbed his ear, and pulled it hard. "Wake up, little pup. That's an order!"

He stood with my grip, a growl starting deep into his chest. "What?" he barked, his teeth elongating into fangs.

I let go of his ear, but only because I had his attention. "Are you really talking to me like that?"

He looked down. His teeth retreated, but his posture was still strong. Defiant. "What do you want?"

"First, you better show me some respect," I said, my voice

firm. "I might not be the alpha anymore, but I'm older than you. Second, you're going for a hunt with me."

He crossed his arms. "I don't want to."

"You don't understand. I'm not giving you an option. You are going with me and that's final." I marched to the door. "Meet me in the back in five minutes. If you don't, I'll barge in here as a wolf and I'll skin you alive. Got it?" He didn't answer. I raised my voice and asked again, "Got it?"

"Yes," he muttered.

I walked out and slammed the door behind me.

What was it with the men in my life? Keeran was being consumed by the power of the amulet, and Wyatt was so depressed that he was a prick and spoke to me as if I were a rat.

The smaller cabins didn't have a proper backyard, just a small patch of grass before the forest started, but it was space enough for me to take off my clothes and shift into my wolf form.

I heard Wyatt's grumbles as he stomped around the cabin, reluctantly getting ready for the hunt. He burst through the door already as a wolf and joined me in the back a moment later.

Good, I told him in his mind. *I was starting to think you really wanted to have your ass handed to you.*

He snorted. *As if you could beat me.*

What? Want to give it a go?

He groaned. *No, thank you. I just want to get this over with so you'll leave me alone again.*

I shook my head. I wouldn't leave him alone after the hunt. If he came back still depressed, I would really beat him up.

I turned to the forest, but something tugged at me. I

scrambled to my folded clothes on the grass, and with my teeth, I pulled out the crystal rose from my pocket. I was getting used to walking around with it, to having it near me, and the thought of leaving it behind didn't sit well with me.

But in wolf form, I didn't have any place to stow it, other than holding the stem between my teeth. I dropped it.

A second later, I picked it up again. With the crystal rose secured between my fangs, I set out into the forest.

Wyatt followed me.

After fifteen minutes of running as fast as we could manage, I sensed a change in Wyatt. It was like his muscles relaxed, even though they were working hard, and his mind cleared a bit.

I knew a damn hunt would do wonders for him, even if it was only for a while.

We found a deer and chased it. Poor animal probably ran away from us, scared for her life, when all Wyatt and I wanted was the thrill of the hunt. We had plenty of food and meat in Unity. We didn't need to kill a deer.

But nothing sent our hearts racing like chasing an animal.

Wyatt and I soon got tired of scaring the poor deer, so we set out on another aimless run. We weaved through the trees, jumped over roots, scurried down valleys, and climbed over hills—all the while keeping a safe distance from Unity.

What's that? Wyatt asked in my mind.

I slowed down and followed his line of sight.

A long line of twisted trees ended in a thick trunk with raised roots—roots that formed what looked like an archway.

I don't know, I answered.

Should we check it out?

As if it had been waiting for Wyatt's question, the rose in my mouth glowed.

What's going on?

I was going to ask you that, Wyatt said.

I explained to him that Keeran had given me the rose, and it was imbued with his magic. Although it hadn't been Keeran's conscious intent, the magic in the rose was supposed to help me when I most needed it.

To test the rose, I took a couple of steps back. Its glow diminished.

Then, I took a few steps forward, in the direction of the archway—the glow intensified.

I think ... I think the rose is trying to show me something, I said.

Let me guess. You want to go through that archway?

You guessed right.

Holding tight to the crystal rose, I strode to the archway. It marked the entrance of a dark cave, but as we went in, the rose's red glow illuminated enough.

The cave wasn't big, but led to another archway and a tunnel.

I hesitated for a second. The rose's glint intensified, almost blinding me.

Okay, okay, I thought to myself as I entered the tunnel.

Dark, narrow, long, winding, and with a stuffy, musky smell.

I don't like this, Wyatt said.

Me neither, I admitted.

I was relieved when the tunnel finally ended, revealing a thin ledge of stone and a deep, vast space all around us.

What is this supposed to be? Wyatt asked.

I didn't know.

I was about to speculate when a faint dark blue glow started in the back of the cave, several feet below our level.

What's that? I wondered.

The dark blue glow shone brighter and brighter, then it spread, as if it had caught on fire. But soon I was able to make out what was happening. There were other tunnels down at the bottom of the cave, and whatever was making that glow was coming through the tunnels.

Could it be one big thing that encompasses the entire cave network? Or several tiny things?

My question was answered moments later when creatures that glowed dark blue stepped out of the tunnels, bathing the cave in their light, and glanced up at me.

Creatures that looked like magical wolves.

"Hello, Luana," a voice echoed.

6

KEERAN

THE MAGIC COURSED THROUGH MY VEINS, AS FAMILIAR AS MY own blood. During the last month, I had trained with my mother almost every day, and despite our constant bickering, I had learned a lot of new tricks.

I couldn't say I was powerful, but I did have more control over my magic.

In this particular session, my mother had created shadow enemies for me to defeat. They had spread out in the clearing, and they moved too fast for me to follow.

But if I focused on my magic, on sharpening my senses, I could clear my sight and see the blur around their edges before and after they moved. I could even see which direction they were going.

Anticipating the movement, I sent a red bolt to my right. I didn't even see any details, until the bolt exploded against the shadow's chest. It burst into thousands of black embers.

"Six down, four to go," I announced, as if my mother wasn't keeping tabs at the edge of the clearing. I just liked to freaking gloat. It wasn't often that I could do that.

The seventh shadow didn't move like the ones before. Instead of practically blinking in and out of existence, this one glided toward me—like a tornado.

I raised a shield to delay it, but the shadow went through it as if it were a wall made of butter.

Summoning a red bolt, I took a few steps back.

Directly into the claws of another shadow.

I was trapped between the two shadow creatures. The one behind me held me down, while the first shadow hovered over me.

Darkness fell over the clearing.

I felt like I was falling into a pit. Drowning in a dark ocean. Lost in an endless abyss.

A claw reached forward, piercing my chest.

I gasped, for a moment panicking and thinking this was real. Then, rage replaced the shock filling my chest. Clenching my fists, I blasted the shadows apart—all of the four left.

There was no darkness now.

Just red.

Red hate, red anger, red fury.

I wanted to find all the shadows in the world and blast them into tiny pieces. I wanted to—

"Keeran."

—squeeze the throat of all the witches who had dared touch me against my will. I wanted to—

"Keeran!"

—burn the world around me and cleanse it of its impurities. I wanted to—

"KEERAN!"

Cold hands clasped my shoulders.

I blinked. The red hot fury faded from my veins. My

sight cleared, and I recognized my mother. She was a few inches in front of, her hands firmly on my shoulders and her brown eyes locked on my face, worry and fear stamped in them.

A pain so sudden and deep cut through my chest. I gasped again, and fell to my knees.

"Keeran, talk to me," my mother said as she knelt in front of me. "What are you feeling? What's happening?"

I took in a deep breath, trying to calm down. "I'm okay," I whispered.

"The hell you are," my mother snapped. "You might be able to hide most of it from Luana and your friends, but you can't hide it from me. I can feel it."

"It's just exhaustion," I lied through gritted teeth. "We have been practicing a lot."

"No, it's not." She pointed to my chest. "It's that damned amulet. Its darkness and power are seeping into you. It's hurting you." She reached for me, but I rose to my feet.

"I'm fine," I snapped.

My mother stood and narrowed her eyes at me. "No, you're not. You won't be fine until that amulet is gone. Please, Keeran, give the amulet to me. I'll find a way to destroy it."

Destroying the amulet meant killing my father with it. I was freaking sick and tired of killing. I had killed so many people in the last couple of years. I couldn't bear doing it again. Especially not my father.

Even if the man was an evil bastard who didn't deserve to stay on this Earth.

That was why I had created the amulet. To imprison him and contain him without the need for killing.

But I could feel it. My father's power, his darkness, flowing from the amulet to me. At the moment, I was okay, but there were times ... there were times when I lost control. When the darkness took over and I only saw red.

Only saw darkness.

"Is there another way to immobilize Soren without killing him?" I asked, my voice rough.

My mother shook her head. "He's a powerful warlock. It's almost impossible to defeat him without landing a killing blow."

"You said almost." It wasn't the first time she had let something like that slip. Once, when I asked her if there was another way to defeat him, she had mentioned there might be, but she didn't elaborate. "You said almost impossible, which means it isn't."

She hesitated. I thought I would have to ask her again. To beg her to tell me. Instead, she let out a long breath. "There's one spell, but it's a fate worse than death."

I frowned. "What do you mean?"

"You might be able to steal Soren's magic."

I stared at her. "Steal his magic?" That sounded so simple. "If it's just that, why haven't others done it? Why haven't you?"

"Because it's a powerful spell," she said. "Although I know how it works, I can't perform one. Actually, as far as I know, there's no witch who can perform it."

"Not even the Queen of All Witches?"

"Aurora might be able to do a temporary version of the spell once she's older and more experienced, but the spell is meant to be cast by a true warlock lord. Your father was the one who created the spell long ago, and he's the only one who was able to perform it successfully."

Successfully. My father had stolen the magic of others. Was that why he was so damn powerful?

"Why do you think I might be able to do it?"

"Because ... you're the true warlock lord. Or you'll be one once your father is gone." She reached forward and pressed her hand on my chest. "I can feel it. The magic, the power. You're strong, almost as strong as Soren ever was."

"I thought the prophecy said I had to kill him to become the warlock lord."

My mother shook her head. "Once his magic is gone, Soren will become a shell, a shadow of himself. He'll be nothing."

"What about the darkness?"

"You won't have killed him, so hopefully, you won't turn evil and you'll be able to keep your sanity."

Hopefully.

It was better than thinking I would turn mad and dark at any minute.

I puffed my chest. "Teach me how to do it."

My mother's brows curled down. "Are you sure you want to learn this, Keeran? It's a dangerous spell."

"If you're worried I'll abuse it, don't. If in the end I can take this amulet off and won't turn evil by killing my father, I won't have a reason to abuse it. I'll just be a normal warlock. That's all I want."

"You'll never be normal," she whispered. I waited for her to argue, but instead, she nodded. "The theory of the spell is easy, the problem is actually having the power to do it." She took several steps back. "All you have to do is focus. Send your magic to me, to my heart, look for where my magic is stored and—"

"Wait." I narrowed my eyes at her. "You want me to try it on you? What if I hurt you?"

"You won't. This will be your first time doing it. You won't be able to sustain it and I'll be fine."

I didn't like it. What if, by some miracle, I pulled it off? What if I lost control again and stole all of her magic? What if I hurt her?

"I don't like this."

My mother's lip tugged in a soft smile. "It's comforting to see you worried about me, but I assure you, I'll be fine." She waved her hand at me. "Now focus. Find where my magic is stored inside me and grab it. Tie a rope around it and pull. That's all you have to do."

Despite the alarm bells in my mind saying that I could not only lose control of my magic, but of myself, of the darkness brewing inside me because of the amulet, I chose to trust my mother.

I closed my eyes, called my power, and concentrated. Like an invisible ray, my magic traveled toward my mother. I hesitated for half a second before sending it inside her.

Her magic was immense and everywhere. She lived and breathed magic. If I had to guess, I would say my mother was similar to Thea in power—like a witch queen. Perhaps that was what she was. Acalla was the witch queen of Unity and her power was testament to that.

However, because of her vast magic, it was hard to find where it all began. But she had given me a hint. Her chest. Her magic probably came from her heart.

Once I knew where to look, it was easy. My mother's magic was an endless well inside her heart.

As instructed, I tied an invisible rope around it and tugged.

My mother gasped.

I loosened the rope. "What is it? Did I hurt you?"

"No, I'm fine. Keep going."

Frowning, I tugged on the rope again. The well didn't

move, but I could feel a sliver of my mother's magic seeping into the rope. I called on it like a child would call a frightened puppy. Slowly, the sliver of magic made its way through the rope.

And right into my hands.

My mother fell on her knees.

"Mom!" I let go of her magic, of my magic too, and ran to her. I held her shoulders before she fell completely to the ground. "What is it? Talk to me!"

She glanced at me, but her vision seemed unfocused. "I'm … fine. I'll be fine." She reached to me and patted my cheek. "You're just stronger than I realized. You were able to steal a little of my magic during your first try. That's incredible."

I looked over her. Other than being exhausted, she didn't seem to be hurt. "I'm sorry." I hadn't meant to steal her magic. I seriously thought I wouldn't be able to perform it so easily. "I don't understand. How could I do it so fast? And why are you so tired?"

"I wasn't resisting because I thought you would need a few tries to actually do it," she said. That explained how easy it was. "As for me, I'm tired because I'm old. My magic is part of me. Having it taken makes me feel like I fought a month-long battle."

I cursed under my breath. "We're not practicing this cursed spell anymore."

She chuckled. "I'm fine, Keeran. All I need is a little rest." She extended her hand to me. "Help me up, please."

Holding her hand, I rose to my feet and pulled her with me. She swayed in place, and I wrapped my arm around her shoulder. "Come on, I'll take you home so you can rest."

My mother offered me a small smile, but didn't resist it. I

practically carried her to her house, and helped her lie down on her bed. I tucked her in and brought her some water.

"I'm just going to close my eyes for a minute," she whispered.

A moment later, she was deep asleep.

I pulled a chair to the side of her bed and sat down. Like a creep, I watched her sleep, a little worried I had taken more than she told me, and she wouldn't wake up.

But as her breathing continued strong as she slept, I relaxed.

The realization that I was genuinely worried about her hit me hard, making me a little breathless. Here I was, taking care of my mother. Never in a million years would I have thought this scenario was possible. First, because I never thought I would meet her, and later, because I hated her for abandoning me.

Spending time with her this past month in Unity had changed things. Seeing her collapse because of my freaking spell had been too hard.

I laid my hand on her bed, right beside hers, and wondered if she and I could be close after all.

7

LUANA

As if by magic, small, round lamps lit up around the cave. The glow from the wolves lessened, and we could see the flat, smooth rock bottom.

A midnight blue wolf, bigger than most, shifted into a tall, broad black human. He had short black hair and seemed older, in his late forties. But the most surprising thing was: He had clothes on! Brown pants and a white tunic and boots. How was that possible?

"I'm Romulus, the leader of the Starlight pack," he said, his voice carrying up the cave walls.

Leader? I asked Wyatt. Why leader? Why not alpha?

That doesn't make sense, Wyatt said.

"I'm sure you have many questions. Please, come down, and I'll explain." Romulus gestured to our side, and sure enough, a narrow stair descended a few steps beside us and hugged the wall until it reached the bottom.

Are you going to trust them? Wyatt asked in my mind. *What if we go down there and they attack? We should just leave.*

I didn't think I could leave, though. We had just found

werewolves that looked like they were made out of pure magic. Even if they were evil in some way, I had to know who they were, how they could be.

More than that, a tug pulled me toward them, and I chose to think this tug was telling me that they could be the allies we needed. If these werewolves joined us in our fight against Isalia, then maybe, just maybe, we had a chance against her and her army.

I need to know, I told Wyatt.

Slowly, I descended the smooth stairs. Like a good friend, Wyatt didn't flinch and came down with me.

At the bottom, the werewolves stepped aside so we could pass. Right in the center, Romulus waited for us. When we approached, a woman in human form stepped forward and held out two long jackets in her hands.

She and Romulus averted their eyes. Around us, all the wolves lowered their heads.

Feeling more self-conscious than usual, I shifted into my human skin and slipped into the jacket. Beside me, Wyatt did the same.

"Thank you for the jackets," I said. I held the crystal rose tight in my hand.

"You're welcome," the woman said, glancing at me. She had short brown hair, deep gray eyes, smooth fair skin, and an easy smile. "I'm Meira, Romulus's mate, and vice-leader of the Starlight pack."

Like magic, all other werewolves turned into their human forms—all of them fully dressed.

I couldn't help by gawk at them.

"I'm sure you have many questions," Romulus repeated, his voice calm, but not kind.

"I don't even know where to start," I whispered as my

mind reeled.

"I know," Wyatt said. His body was tense beside me, as if he was ready for a fight. "Why do you call yourself a leader, and not an alpha?"

"Because I'm not the true alpha of this pack," Romulus said, unflinching. I had the impression that he would answer all of our questions, even the most absurd ones, with strength and grace. "I'm just leading it until our rightful alpha returns to us."

I frowned. "But ... that doesn't make sense. An alpha is a wolf who either wins a challenge from the previous alpha, or steps up after the alpha dies."

"Not in the Starlight pack," Meira said. "As you can see, we're a little different from a normal werewolf pack."

"Our alpha is a direct descendants of the wolf gods," Romulus explained. "Because of that, the alpha mantle is passed through blood, not by force."

"The alpha shares his magic with the rest of the pack," Meira continued. "Thus granting us unique abilities."

"Like glowing in the dark," I muttered.

She chuckled. "Among many other things."

"Wait." Wyatt raised his index finger. "If you don't have an alpha, how do you still have magic?"

"The magic is bestowed to the wolf by the alpha right after birth," Romulus said. "Most wolves you see here got their magic from our late alpha."

"The ones who were born since then are mostly like normal werewolves," Meira said, the tone in her voice ringing with sadness. I glanced around. "You won't see them now. They are younger and less powerful. Whenever we have a stranger entering our cave, something that rarely happens, they stay out of sight."

That made sense, though I couldn't imagine how it felt for the younger wolves to be different from their parents and friends.

"I'm assuming Almae knows you're in Unity's territory?" I asked.

Romulus nodded. "After our alpha and his family were murdered, our pack broken and our territory lost, Almae found us roaming and hiding in the forest not long after she founded Unity." He opened her arms wide. "We created these tunnels with her help."

Hiding. They had been hiding for years now. I doubted I could recruit them to join me in the war against Isalia.

"You called Luana by her name," Wyatt said suddenly.

I had been so entranced in their magic, I had forgotten that. "That's true. How do you know my name?"

"Because Almae made a prophecy a few year ago," Meira said.

"In her prophecy, Almae foresaw that the child of our previous alpha hadn't been killed as we first thought," Romulus said. "She had been merely lost and misguided. In time, she would return to us, but her magic would be gone and she wouldn't look like us."

I tilted my head. "Who ...?"

I gasped.

My father had been the alpha of a forgotten pack. He and my mother had been killed by Isalia. She would have killed me too if I hadn't been whisked away. I had forgotten all about that until recently.

"It's you, Luana." Romulus's eyes were fixed on mine, but despite all that he had told me, he didn't seem happy about having found his alpha's lost heir. "I can feel our magic in you, locked away. The moment you stepped through the archway outside the cave, I was sure you were our rightful alpha."

I was their alpha.

By the moon, could it be this simple? Me, the alpha of a powerful, magical wolf pack? With them by my side, I could easily defeat Isalia and her army.

I shook with anticipation and excitement.

But something was wrong.

"If … if I'm your rightful alpha, why don't I feel anything?" I glanced down at my hands. "Why don't I feel the alpha's magic at work? Why can't I turn into a glowing wolf like you?"

Romulus shook his head. "I don't know."

"Our guess is that either your foster parents found a way to block the magic inside you, or the trauma you lived through blocked it," Meira said. "Either way, to become the alpha of the Starlight pack and have a bond with us, you have to be able to access your magic."

I stared at them. "How do I do that?"

Romulus and Meira shared a knowing look.

"There is a way," Meira started.

"But it won't be easy," Romulus added.

"Tell us what it is," Wyatt said. He sounded as eager as I felt. "If there's a way, I'm sure Luana can do it, no matter what."

His faith in me was so comforting, it brought a small smile to my lips.

"You must find three objects," Romulus said. "The mirror of all seeing, the dagger of all hunting, and the crown of all branches."

"These three objects can tap into the pack's magic since they were once gifted to us by the wolf gods themselves," Meira said. "Unfortunately, they were lost a long time ago."

"Where do I find them?" I asked.

"We don't know," Meira said. "If we knew, we would already have these objects with us."

They were sending me to find a specific seed in the entire forest. That didn't help at all.

Wyatt frowned. "I have another question. Why are you doing this? Why not just continue as leader of the pack? Why the need to find your alpha?"

"Wyatt!" I felt embarrassed by his harsh tone. It was like he was accusing them of a crime.

"I'm serious," Wyatt continued. "Have you ever seen a leader who wanted to relinquish his power? We've met several rulers and none of them wanted to give up their throne."

"That's a good question," Romulus said. "Maybe other races aren't like us, but the Starlight wolves are loyal to their pack, especially to their alpha and the alpha's family. Perhaps it's the magic in our veins, or that we were blessed by the wolf gods, but we feel honor and loyalty differently than most. We are truer than most."

"When Almae told us you were alive and well ..." Meira's eyes brimmed with unshed tears. "We couldn't believe it. We were so happy that we wanted to go after you right then."

I frowned. I hadn't thought of that. "Why didn't you?"

"Because Almae's prophecy wasn't specific," Romulus said. "We didn't know where you were, how old you were then, and even your name. It was only a few weeks ago, when you first visited Unity, that the rumors of a new she-wolf reached our ears. We then learned your name."

"But you left," Meira explained. "So we thought it wasn't you after all."

"Until you walked in this cave and we all felt it." Romulus

rested a hand over his heart. "It's a weak feeling, because of your locked magic, but it's there nonetheless."

"All you need to do now is find the objects and come back to us," Meira said.

I swallowed hard, deciding I couldn't keep it all to myself. "Do you know about my fight against Isalia, the she-wolf who killed my parents?"

Romulus nodded. "We learned it was her who murdered your parents and destroyed our territory only a few weeks ago, but yes, we do know now."

I held my breath. "Once I recover the items and become your alpha, will you help me defeat her?"

Romulus lifted his finger to his face and traced the shape of a crescent moon on his forehead. The moon's shape glowed dark blue for a moment, then disappeared.

"I will," he said, with a faint smile. "That's a promise."

Meira took her finger to her forehead and repeated the gesture. Then, the other wolves did the same. The glow on their foreheads was proof of their loyalty. It warmed my heart.

"Thank you," I whispered.

8

KEERAN

AFTER SLEEPING FOR ONLY A COUPLE OF HOURS, ACALLA GOT UP from bed saying she had things to do and problems to solve. She still looked pale and frail, which was apparent as she reached for the doorknob with shaking hands, or when she tried to walk down the hall and wobbled on her feet.

I argued she should go back to bed.

"I'm fine," she insisted.

I relented, but only an inch. She could get out of bed, but she had to stay seated in the living room, reading a book, painting, playing a game—as long as she relaxed and rested a little.

She tried to argue about that too, but I wasn't having it.

At some point, she realized I was serious and stayed put. She sat on the couch with her feet up on the coffee table, grabbed a book from the end table, and flipped it open.

To pass the time, I made her some tea.

But soon, I was bored again. The air only grew more awkward when we tried to fill it with casual talk.

When she finally fell asleep in her bed, I thought my mother and I were finally crossing the longest bridge toward the mending of our relationship.

Now that I didn't seem to be able to stay seated beside her, I wasn't so sure.

At some point in the afternoon, I went to check on Farrah and Wyatt. Those two had been quieter than mice since we first arrived, but I couldn't blame them. Wyatt was still dealing with the trauma of all he had done while under my father's spell, and Farrah watched over him.

To my surprise, Farrah was alone in the cabin.

"Thank the snow, Luana was able to take Wyatt out for a run," she said. "I hope that helps clear his mind a little."

I hoped so too. I stayed with Farrah for a few minutes, but she was getting ready to help at the infirmary. According to Acalla, not many people got sick or hurt in Unity, and most supernaturals had speedy healing as one of their powers, but when someone got sick, it meant trouble. Thankfully, nobody was sick this time, but Farrah was trying to learn all she could from the healers, so she could be useful, just in case.

Without much to do, and already a little worried about her, I went back to my mother's house.

I found her in the same spot, with a book in her lap, but this time, her head was against the back of the couch, and her eyes were closed. The slow up and down of her chest confirmed she was only sleeping.

I sat down on the chair across the coffee table and watched over her.

She looked old and frail like this. An instinct to protect her rose in me, and I didn't know what to make of it.

Why would I protect the woman who had abandoned

me? Who knew I was alive, in the midst of evil witches, who had created a paradise and never went back for me? She had the perfect life here, and apparently, she hadn't wanted her son to mess with it.

Now, I was here, raining on her parade. She must hate me even more now than when she first abandoned me.

A sliver of rage stirred in my chest. Soon, the darkness followed. I could feel it, but I couldn't fight it. The darkness was stronger than me, and once it sank its claws in me, there wasn't much I could do.

Before I threw a bolt of magic at my sleeping mother, I pushed up from the armchair and marched to the backyard.

I took in a lungful of fresh air, but it wasn't enough to assuage my anger and the darkness within me. I was falling into their endless pit, and one of these days, I wouldn't be able to crawl out of it.

Two wolves burst through the forest, and I called my magic.

"Hey, it's us," Wyatt said, after he shifted into his human form.

I pulled back my power, but being startled like that only added to my irritation.

Beside him, Luana shifted too. She smiled at me. "You won't believe what just happened."

I understood the whole feeling okay with nakedness thing, but I really didn't like having my mate naked beside another man, especially when he was nude too.

"One sec," I muttered, before walking into my mother's cabin. Careful not to make any noise, I grabbed two throw blankets from the living room. Back outside, I flung them at Luana and Wyatt. "Here."

"Thanks." Luana wrapped the blanket around herself.

"Luana, tell him before I do," Wyatt said as he circled the blanket around his waist. It was better, but not by much.

I groaned. "What is it?"

Luana's smile faltered. "I ... Are you okay?"

I crossed my arms. "I'm perfect."

She narrowed her eyes at me. Even if I tried to hide my anger and irritation, she could hear the rapid beating of my heart and my sharp exhales. "What happened?"

"I'm going to check on Farrah," Wyatt mumbled before walking away.

I stared at Luana, as if challenging her for ... what?

"Keeran, tell me what happened, please." Her voice was calm and stable. So unlike the hotheaded wolf she was.

"Nothing." I jerked my chin toward her. "But something happened to you and you wanted to tell me about it."

"Well, yes, but if you don't want to talk right now, it can wait."

"We can talk now."

Luana tilted her head. She stared at me, probably considering what was best. Telling me even if I didn't care, or not telling me and making me more irritated by hiding something from me.

It was a freaking impossible choice.

Luana let out a long breath. "I found a group of magical wolves hidden in Unity's forest. They are called the Starlight pack, and they glow dark blue in the dark. They told me that my father was their alpha."

More supernaturals hidden in Unity, and this time, it was the wolves from Luana's pack. My mother's treachery seemed endless. "And?"

She flinched. "Aren't you glad I found my pack?"

I shrugged. I didn't care if she was the alpha of the red or blue or green pack, as long as we found more allies. "Will they help us against Isalia?"

"That's the catch," she said. I wasn't even aware there was a catch. "Somehow, I lost my magic and I can only be their alpha if I get it back."

I frowned. Wolves with magic. I wasn't sure how I felt about that. I had only known I had magic for two years, and I was still getting used to it. Now my mate, who was supposed to be a freaking werewolf, was telling me she had magic?

Jealousy joined the anger and irritation swirling inside me.

"Get back your magic," I muttered, trying hard to not blow on her. "How do you do that?"

"I need to find three objects," she said, the eagerness taking over her voice. "The mirror of all seeing, the dagger of all hunting, and the crown of all branches. They were gifts from the gods, passed on by my bloodline, but somehow they have been lost."

"The mirror of what?" My irritation was about to blow. "Those names are ridiculous. How do you know these glow-in-the-dark wolves aren't just playing with you?"

Her brows curled down. "I don't—"

The backdoor opened and my mother walked out. "They aren't playing with Luana. They have been waiting for their rightful alpha for many years now."

She was still pale, but that didn't matter when she was butting in on my conversation with my mate.

"You knew who they were, and you kept them hidden all these years?" I snapped. "Why the hell didn't you tell Luana? Oh, wait, I know. Keeping Unity hidden is more important."

Taken aback, my mother stared at me before continuing.

"I didn't know who their alpha was, or where she was. They just wanted a place to stay while they regrouped and waited. Seeing as their intention was peaceful, I offered them a place to stay. That was all."

Should I believe her? She had lied about so many things. I didn't know if any words out of her mouth could ever be true.

"Almae, have you ever heard about the mirror of all seeing, the dagger of all hunting, and the crown of all branches?" Luana asked, ignoring my fuming face.

"Rumor had it, your father had one of those objects," my mother said. "The mirror of all seeing."

"Really?" Luana's brows hitched up. "Where could that be?"

"The rumors told of a crystal cave outside the Starlight pack territory, about a half-day walk from here, and that your father had the mirror hidden there."

"You just said it was rumors," I snapped.

My mother threw me a cold look. "All rumors have a hint of truth."

"There's only one way to find out." Luana tightened the blanket around herself. "I'll leave for the cave tomorrow at first light."

I scoffed. "Luana, think about it. Acalla said it was a rumor. You're going to lose an entire day, walking around, trying to find a cursed cave?"

Luana gritted her teeth. "Do you have a better idea?"

"Yes," I spat. "Do some research before throwing yourself into a senseless search."

"Keeran, don't say that," my mother said. "This is important to Luana."

I pointed a finger at my mother. "You stay out of this!"

She flinched before whispering, "I give up." After a sorrowful glance at Luana, Acalla walked back into her house.

"Keeran, your mother wants to help," Luana said. "Don't be mean to her."

What the hell? Now she was patronizing me too? "She deserves it."

"That damn amulet. It's poisoning you. Please take it off so we can talk."

I reached for the amulet, cradling it in my hand. "You know I can't take it off." Despite that, I didn't want to take it off. "I'm fine."

Luana shook her head, her eyes full of anguish. "I can't talk to you like this."

She spun on her heels and stomped away.

"Where the hell do you think you're going?" I yelled at her.

But Luana didn't slow down. She didn't even glance my way as she walked away.

From me.

I bumped a closed fist against my chest. Too much built up inside—anger, irritation, jealousy, and now disappointment—threatening to explode.

In tandem with my temper, my magic warmed in my veins, asking for release.

I considered running into the forest to blow up bushes or trees to burn off some of this pent-up energy, but I decided to take another route. I closed my eyes and focused. I calmed my breathing, I reared back my magic, and I pushed down my temper.

It took a while, but I won this round.

A long, slow exhale flew out my lips, and I opened my eyes.

What the hell had I done?

9

LUANA

THE WORST PART ABOUT HAVING A FIGHT WITH KEERAN IN THE evening was going to bed alone and worrying about him the entire night. I tossed and turned in bed, concerned about what he might be doing.

Finally, at around three in the morning, I heard as he tiptoed into the cabin—his heartbeat and breathing almost back to normal—and lay down on the couch in the living room.

At least he had the decency of not pushing his luck by trying to come to bed.

Despite having him back, I didn't relax. The little I slept was light and restless. But determined to follow through with my new quest, I got up at first light and got dressed.

Last night, Almae had brought me a detailed map of Unity and the surrounding areas. She didn't know how far I would have to go to find the crystal cave, but she was confident I could see all the caves on the map in a half-day hike.

I had also talked to Wyatt and Farrah last night. In a much better mood, Wyatt had offered to go with me on this mission, but since Farrah had already asked him to help her with some things in town, I told him to stay. Perhaps the excitement of going after the mirror would keep him in a better mood, but I also knew Farrah was perfectly capable of doing that. Besides, as far as I knew, they hadn't spent much quality time together because of Wyatt's depression. He was feeling better now, so he had to take advantage of that and spend his good days with her.

They might not know it, or at least admit it, but they liked each other, and to me, there was nothing more obvious than that.

Since I didn't know what I would encounter during my hike, I rolled up a long T-shirt around the crystal rose, and prepared a thin leather tie. Once I wolfed out, I would ask Almae to tie the shirt and rose to my leg, so I could take them with me—at least, it would be easier than carrying both items between my teeth.

I reached for the knob and heard as Keeran stirred on the couch.

Shit, I had hoped to sneak out of the house before he woke up. Truth was, I knew he hadn't slept well either.

I sighed and walked out of the bedroom.

Keeran stood from the couch and smoothed his hands through his messy hair. "You're up. Good morning."

"Morning." I barely glanced his way as I walked around the kitchen's tall counter. I wasn't in the mood for a big breakfast. I would just grab something, shove it in my mouth, and be done with it.

"Luana." Keeran followed me into the kitchen. "I want to apologize for yesterday. I don't know what came over me and I was—"

I spun around and glared at him. "You don't know what

came over you? I know." I pointed at his chest, where I could see the small bulge of the amulet under his black shirt. "This came over you."

He balled his fists and I braced myself, sure he would verbally attack me again. "Can we not talk about the amulet right now? I'm trying to apologize."

"You're not doing a good job." I turned and reached for the wicker basket full of bagels.

Keeran grabbed my wrist and gently pulled me back. "Luana, please. I'm sorry. Really, I'm sorry. I don't want to fight anymore."

I jerked my hand free from his grip and crossed my arms. "What do you want to do, then?"

"I want to help you," he said simply. "I want to go to this crystal cave with you and search for the mirror." I blinked, sure I wasn't hearing him right. "If this mirror is important to you, then it's important to me too."

My shoulders deflated and the fight fled me. "Are you sure? You won't nag me about it the entire way, or complain about it being a silly quest."

His eyes fixed on mine, Keeran stepped into my space and cupped my face. "I'm really sorry for being a jerk yesterday. I love you, Luana, and I want to help you."

The corner of my lips tugged up, but before I could fully smile, Keeran's mouth crashed into mine.

I didn't even try to hold on to my disappointment and anger. There was no need to. Deep down, I knew it hadn't been him. Keeran was a good man through and through. He would never intentionally be mean to me. Glad his senses had come back, I let all the hurt go and melted into his kiss. I wound my arms around him and held him tight against me.

"This is much better," I whispered against his lips.

"Agreed," he muttered before deepening the kiss. He pushed me back, until my butt hit the counter. He broke the kiss and looked at me. "I think we'll be a little late, though."

"It'll be worth it." I grabbed his collar and pulled him back to me.

MY MORNING HADN'T STARTED AS I PLANNED, BUT I HAD TO admit it had been much better. Making up with Keeran, and making love to him, was better than anything else.

But in the end, we had to come back to reality and face the day. We ate a light breakfast, packed for a day's journey, and left Unity with the sun already halfway up in the sky.

I had resisted shifting, but Keeran had assured me his magic had grown and he could maintain a running spell longer. I shifted and ran as a wolf, while Keeran zipped through the forest by my side.

When I thought we were near the area Almae had told me about, I asked Keeran to check the map. We followed the map to the nearest cave. Then to the next one. The next one. And the next one.

In two hours, we checked over fifteen caves in the region, and none of them was the crystal cave.

Tired of searching for the needle in the haystack, I shifted and sat down on the grassy ground beside a thin stream that cut through the forest. Acting like a gentleman, Keeran put his cloak over my shoulders and sat down beside me.

The fairy tale was short-lived.

Keeran grunted. "I knew this was a mistake."

I glanced at him, doing my best to rein in my temper. An

irritable warlock and a hotheaded werewolf. If we ended up arguing again, I wasn't sure what would happen.

"There are still a lot of caves to check." I cupped a handful of water from the stream and drank it. "We can't say it's a mistake yet."

"Luana, think about it. A crystal cave? It's ridiculous."

"Have you ever stopped to consider what the humans think of us? When a human mentions magic, or werewolves, or vampires, they think it's fantasy. All ridiculous. Yet, here we are." I paused. "We've seen so much; we've done so much. Why would a crystal cave be ridiculous in our world?"

"Because!" He groaned. "I don't know … it just sounds too good to be true. We find a crystal cave, find a mysterious mirror that was hidden there, and suddenly, you're the alpha of a magical werewolf pack?"

"It's not suddenly!" My temper flared up. "It's my birthright. I was born in that magical lineage. Somehow, I lost my magic, but I want to get it back. Everything will be so much easier if I can get it back." Being powerful, having a pack, fighting Isalia alongside them. Belonging somewhere.

"I'm just saying, you shouldn't get your hopes up." His words were meant to be calm and comforting, but the sharp edge to his voice grated. "For all we know, these are rumors."

I shot up to my feet. "Well, I'm going to find it just to prove to you it wasn't a rumor."

I stomped away before our argument turned into a real fight.

After grunting again, Keeran followed me.

This time, I remained in my human form while checking the next few caves—all normal caves, without a trace of crystals.

Another hour passed. The sun had curved the top of the

sky and had started its slow descent. I was starting to worry Keeran was right. What if the crystal cave was a rumor and I never found the mirror of all seeing?

We were coasting the bottom of a steep hill when a red glow caught my eye. I turned to Keeran, and sure enough, the rose, which was peeking from underneath the flap of the small satchel he carried, was glowing.

"This is it." I grabbed the rose. "We're near the crystal cave."

Keeran looked at the map. "But there aren't any caves around here."

"A cave like this wouldn't be on any maps," I said, realizing we had been going about this all wrong. Even in the supernatural world, who would put a place that was supposed to be hidden on a map?

"You mean we've just wasted the last three hours?"

I ignored his question and his bitter tone. Instead, I held the rose tight in my hand and extended my arm. The glow became brighter. "It's over here." I used the rose as a compass and followed it as it guided us to a wall of dirt and rock on the side of the hill. The rose shone more, and I had to avert my eyes because of its intense glow. I lowered the rose and reached forward with my other hand. My hand disappeared inside the dirt wall. On instinct, I pulled my hand back and gasped. "It's here." I stepped through the wall.

"Luana!"

At first, it was dark, as if I had crossed into a black hole. Then, the colors exploded through the darkness, almost blinding me. I brought a hand up to protect my eyes, but the adjustment was fast.

I blinked, trying to take in how beautiful and fantastical this cave was.

Keeran stepped through the portal. "What the—?"

"It's amazing," I whispered.

The cave was like a huge auditorium, wide and high in the back, narrowing and low toward the stage, where in this case was an archway, with wide steps leading the way. But the most magnificent part was the crystals lining the walls, the floor, and the ceiling. Blue, pink, orange, green ... so many colors mixed, like a rainbow had splat all over this place.

Enamored, I went down step by step, taking my time to observe and commit the imagines to memory. Behind me, Keeran seemed bored as hell.

I took one last glance around the magical place before crossing beneath the archway.

I stepped through and instantly the colors and lights were gone, replaced by darkness. A red flame appeared beside me.

"I think we'll need this," Keeran said, extending his hand in front of us so the flame floating on his palm illuminated the place.

But there wasn't much to see. We were in a dark tunnel, just a little taller than us, and wide enough for the two of us to stand side by side. That was it.

"I'm guessing we have to follow the tunnel," I said.

"I don't like it," Keeran mumbled.

What other choice did I have? Go back empty-handed? Just the fact that we had found the hidden crystal cave was proof that we were meant to be here. That I was meant to find the mirror.

"Come on," I muttered.

I took a step forward.

The ground crumbled under my foot. I jumped back as the walls shook. A pit opened, swallowing the ground. Keeran held on to me and pulled me back against him.

When the walls stopped shaking and the pit stopped expanding, Keeran and I took in the new challenge: There was a huge hole in the ground. It was over thirty feet long, which meant I couldn't wolf out and jump across. Could I climb down and back up? Careful, I leaned over the edge of the pit and looked down.

I couldn't see the bottom.

"Here." Keeran grabbed a small pebble from the ground and imbued it with red light. Then, he dropped it on the pit.

The pebble went down and down and down.

And down.

We stopped seeing the pebble's red glow, but we never heard it reaching the bottom.

"Well, climbing into the pit is out of question," I said.

Keeran frowned. "I'm starting to think this place is full of booby traps."

He was right. "It's a test," I muttered. "If you can make it through the booby traps, then you're worthy of the mirror."

"With my magic, this will be easy." He walked to the edge of the pit. "I'll just conjure a bridge."

"No," I said. "I appreciate the offer, but this was made for a werewolf, one probably without magic. As the rightful alpha, I should reach the mirror using my skills. Please, don't interfere."

"Excuse me? I came all this freaking way to help you, and now you're asking me to just sit back and relax while you're almost killed by traps?"

I took a step closer to him and put my hands on his shoulders. "I really appreciate your help, but more than your help, I appreciate you being here. You can keep me company and cheer me on while I go through the traps." Only the moon knew how many there would be. "But please, do not interfere."

"I don't like this."

"It's okay." I rose to my tiptoes and pressed my lips to his in a quick peck. "It'll be a breeze. You'll see."

I took off his cloak and returned it to him. Then, I shifted.

As fast as I could, I jumped to the wall on the right, fitting my paws on small indentions on the surface, and advancing toward the other side. But my center of gravity was tilted, and I felt my weight dragging me down. When I was a few feet from the other side, I pushed hard against the wall and leaped as far as I could. My front paws landed all right, but my hind paws scurried over the overhang. Dirt loosened, making it hard for me to grind my claws and gain footing. But I didn't stop fighting.

I was dragged down a little more. Scrambling, I felt a small rock jutting out of the cliff wall. I used it to propel me forward. I pushed and jumped.

I rolled on the ground, taking a deep breath.

A moment later, Keeran was beside me. "Are you all right?" The red glow of his magical bridge shone behind him.

Show off.

I got up on all fours and nodded.

Carefully, I trudged forward. A spike jutted up from the ground, and I sprang back, avoiding it by inches. Spikes suddenly shot out from the ground in rapid succession.

Then, they were gone.

I waited, but they didn't come back.

I took a step forward again—and the first spike came out. Then the others.

Trying to make note of a pattern, I did that for a couple more times. The stakes were close together, and they moved too fast, but there was one way, one narrow space where I could weave through them, just enough for a slim wolf.

I prepared myself and pressed against the ground again. The stakes appeared, and I rushed through them, squeezing my body through the path. I was almost out of them, when I stepped on a loose pebble and lost my footing. A spike grazed my leg, and I let out a yelp.

I stomped forward and away from the spikes.

Once more, Keeran appeared by my sides a few seconds later. "Let me see," he said, kneeling beside me.

It hadn't been much. Just a nasty scratch and a little blood. I ignored him and strode forward. But Keeran close his hand around my leg and cursed under his breath. "I said, let me see it, damn it."

He sounded angry.

I didn't care. There was no reason to stop and look at a scratch when I was almost at the first item I needed from my list.

With a little force, I drove farther into the tunnel. Keeran let me go. His exasperated exhale reached my ears.

If he was going to be this ridiculous, then he shouldn't have come.

I kept going, always on the lookout for more traps.

Ahead, the ground and tunnel's walls were wider and smoother. I halted right before this change. Two large, dark blue wolves appeared. Their bodies shimmered as if they were made of smoke and magic.

The only thing I could think of was that I needed to fight them.

Without thinking, I raced toward them. The two wolves turned to me and we fought. They hit me hard, but when I tried hitting them, my hand passed through their bodies as if they were ghosts.

What in the moon?

I worked up a sweat as I dodged their attacks and thought of how I was going to defeat them. Nothing I did, nothing I attempted, worked. I was at a loss.

Then, when I turned and had them between Keeran and me, I saw it. Their bodies shimmered with the light projecting from the flame over Keeran's hand.

Which gave me an idea.

Weaving past the two wolves, I raced toward Keeran. "What is it?" he asked.

I didn't have time to waste by shifting into my human form, then into a wolf again. Instead, I tugged on his sleeve, and he lowered his arm, turning his hand over. "The light? You want me to put out the light?"

I nodded.

He did as I asked.

The light was gone, and the tunnel was pitch black. I moved forward, across the smooth patch of stone, bracing myself for the wolves to attack me, but nothing happened. The wolves were gone. The ground changed beneath my paws, and I let out a yelp. Keeran conjured a flame again, illuminating the tunnel.

"Good thinking," he said, though he didn't sound pleased.

Together, we walked down the tunnel.

Until it came to a dead end.

A rock wall greeted us. Despair rushed through my veins. That was it? All of those booby traps for nothing? Was this a trick?

Behind me, Keeran muttered his discontent, but I focused on the quest. This had to be another obstacle, another trap.

What if it wasn't?

I stepped forward and rested my head on the damn wall.

My paw moved down, as if I had pressed broken tile.

But it was much more than that.

Starting from the bottom, blue light cut through the wall, revealing an opening. The wall slid open in two panels—a hidden door.

Holding my breath, I walked into a large, round chamber with heavy, stale air. Blue lights ran the perimeter of the room, illuminating the area.

The small pear-shaped mirror with delicate silver framing stood on a wooden stand in the middle of the room.

I shifted into my human body and advance toward the stand. With shaking hands, I reached for the mirror.

And picked it up easily.

"I got it," I whispered incredulously. Cradling the light mirror in my hands, I turned to Keeran. "I got it."

Keeran glanced at our surroundings, waiting for another bobby trap to spring. "Is this it? Are you done?"

"I guess so," I said.

He walked closer and looked over the mirror. "That little thing is the mighty mirror of all seeing?" He scrunched his nose. "I can feel a little magic, but it doesn't seem powerful."

"It doesn't matter. As long as it helps me become the true Starlight pack alpha, and eventually defeat Isalia, that's all the matters."

The mirror's surface shone.

I lowered it and looked at its face. I gasped upon seeing the reflection of Isalia, leaning against a big, dark wood chair in a dimly lit room.

Her belly was round and swollen.

Then, the image was gone, and the light faded.

"What happened?" Keeran asked, looking at the mirror.

"I don't know." I paused and thought for a moment. "We mentioned Isalia's name." The mirror of all seeing. Seeing. "I think ... this mirror can show us anyone we want."

"Try it again," Keeran said.

"Isalia," I said. This time, the mirror didn't work. "That's odd."

Keeran snickered. "What a useless trinket." He jerked his head toward the entrance. "Come on, let's go back. I'm tired."

He walked back to the tunnel.

And I stayed in my spot for a moment, thinking about Keeran's terrible mood swings and how much longer I could endure them. I had to find out more about this mirror's powers.

But I could do that in Unity.

Rushing my steps, I caught up with Keeran and went back with him.

10

KEERAN

IN THE MOONLIGHT, LUANA AND I SNEAKED INTO UNITY THE same way we had come out, but as we headed to our cabin, we saw people running down the roads, toward the marketplace.

Still wearing only my cloak, Luana stopped two witches. "What's happening?"

The older witch stared at us with big eyes. "Haven't you heard? A stranger was found outside Unity. A warlock."

"What?" I asked, almost dropping the mirror.

"He was trying to break in," the younger one said. "But Almae caught him. She's holding him in the infirmary right now."

"Thanks," I muttered. The women dashed away, and I turned to Luana. "We should check it out."

"I agree, but not with the mirror." She took the mirror from me. "I'll drop this off and put on some clothes. Go help your mother. I'll be right there."

I nodded once then ran down the road toward the marketplace. The number of supernaturals flocking the road increased the closer I got, but there was a real sea of people in front of the infirmary.

As expected, I was recognized right away, and the supernaturals let me pass. "Thank you," I muttered, before reaching the door and opening it.

I practically jumped inside and closed the door again.

The infirmary was a simple place: a large room with a desk and some couches in the corner, and several stretchers separated by curtains in the rest of the space.

This time, though, there was a chair in the middle of the room, and a warlock was tied to it.

"Talk!" Acalla shouted. Standing in front of the chair, she extended her hand to him. "Tell me who sent you here and why, or I'll make you wish you were dead."

Laughter bubbled out of the warlock's mouth as he jerked against the ropes around his chest, wrists, and ankles. "I'll never tell you anything. You better just get this over with and kill me."

A white bolt appeared in Acalla's hand.

"Mother," I called.

The bolt faded away and she turned to me with wide eyes. "Keeran, you're here."

I walked up to her. "What happened?"

"I caught this warlock trying to break into Unity about an hour ago," she said, her dark eyes fixed on the warlock. "Do you know him?"

I had been staring at him since I had entered the infirmary, but I couldn't place him. If he had been one of Soren's warlocks, he had been a quiet one, because I didn't remember him.

I shook my head. "Never seen him before."

"I've seen you," the warlock said, a sly grin on his lips.

I approached him. "When? Where?"

"Don't bother," my mother said. "I've been asking questions for an hour now, and he hasn't said a word."

"I just didn't want to talk to you," the warlock said. "But I might talk to my lord's son."

So, he was one of Soren's warlocks.

I crossed my arms. "How do you know me, and what are you doing here?"

"Soren has many warlocks, serving as spies or doing other odd jobs for our lord, and all of us know who our lord's son is." His gaze fell to the amulet hanging from my chest. "We all know you're holding our lord prisoner." His eyes darkened. "I've come to free him."

I snorted. The warlock was tied down with magic imbued ropes, with Acalla and I watching over him. Not to mention the many supernaturals waiting outside this door. Did he really think he would be able to touch me? To get the amulet? Or even to escape this place in one piece?

No, he hadn't come to escape. He had come on a suicide mission. He knew this was a one-shot thing. He would try to liberate his lord, but he was sure he would die in the process.

My mother pulled me back a few steps and whispered, "I don't like this. We need to do something."

"Are you suggesting we kill him?" That word, that act, stirred something in me. Something deep, something dark. I was sure many would die during our fight with Isalia, but I wouldn't gratuitously kill a defenseless man.

"I have a better idea," Acalla said, her voice devoid of emotion. "You should steal his magic."

A cold chill ran down my spine. "W-what?"

"That's a way of dealing with him without killing him.

Also, it's good practice for when you need to take Soren's magic."

I shook my head. "I don't like it."

"Keeran, my son." She sighed. "It's not like we have many choices here. I won't risk keeping him alive. If he escaped, Unity would be in danger." Again, she was only worried about Unity. "Either I kill him, or you steal his magic."

I hated this. I hated having to choose between the lesser of two evils. I hated that the choice rested solely on me.

But she was right. We couldn't keep him alive, but I certainly didn't want to kill him.

There was no choice here.

I groaned. "I'll do it. I'll steal his magic."

My mother patted my shoulder. "Good." She retreated, giving me plenty of space.

Taking a deep breath, I faced the warlock and channeled my magic.

His eyes widened. "What are you doing?"

I didn't answer. I focused on the spell. Like I had done before with Acalla, I sent my magic to him, but unlike her, who had made it easy for me, he had a thick barrier around himself.

I pushed my magic, probing and poking, trying to find an opening. In a matter of seconds, sweat beaded my forehead and my breathing trembled with the effort.

"Stop it!" the warlock shouted. "Whatever the hell you're doing, stop it!"

I couldn't stop it. I had to do this.

Finally, my magic broke through the barrier, and rolled into a sea of power—of dark magic. This man was almost as powerful as my mother, but in a different way. Where my mother's power was pure and light, this man's energy was heavy and evil.

Like my father's.

Groaning, I guided my magic through his veins, his muscles, his core, looking for the source. I found the thick, heavy ball in his gut. I wrapped my magic around it and tugged. The warlock fought me, and at first, it didn't budge.

"Stop it!" the warlock screamed.

I sent more of my magic into in him and grabbed the source with all I had. The warlock screamed as the ball moved past his stomach. I pulled the ball up his chest, through his throat.

"No!"

The warlock clamped his mouth down, as if the gesture would be enough to contain his power's core. In a last attempt, he called on his magic, holding on tooth and nail. The moment he got hold of a sliver, he blasted it at me.

Surprised by the sudden energy, I jumped back to avoid being hit, dropping my magical hold on him. The spell was gone. I had failed to steal his magic.

With a roar, the warlock broke the ropes around him and sent a rainfall of strikes at my mother and me. My mother created a shield in front of us. But this warlock was more powerful than I first thought. He sent a powerful strike, breaking the shield and sending us flying backward.

I hit the wall hard, and I had to take a second to catch my breath.

A couple of feet to my side, my mother was crouched on the ground.

"Mother?" I went to her. "Are you okay?"

She lifted her head, her eyes unfocused. "Where is he?"

I glanced up. The warlock was nowhere to be seen.

Screams echoed from outside.

I ran out.

People were scattered, cowering behind the stands.

"Where is he?" I shouted.

A witch stepped forward and pointed in the direction of the lake with a shaking hand. "He went that way."

Groaning, I ran after him.

"Keeran, stop." My mother's voice was clear and firm. I turned and faced her. "You should stay here." A group of vampires, werewolves, warlocks, and fae came through the marketplace. They had the same brooch on their shirts—the official guards of Unity. "Go after him. Catch him alive, if you can. If you can't catch him, kill him."

The men nodded once, then marched away.

I stalked to my mother. "I'm going after him!"

"Keeran, everyone is watching," she said in a low voice. "Let's talk about this somewhere else." She turned to the crowd. "The rest of you, go to your houses. Stay there until you hear it's safe to come out."

Whispers filled the air.

"What will happen?"

"Isn't Unity safe anymore?"

"What do we do now?"

"If Unity isn't safe, we should move."

My mother ignored the harsh words as people scattered to their houses, and told me, "Come on."

⁂

ACALLA PACED THE LIVING ROOM. HER HANDS SHOOK, AND SHE groaned every two seconds. She looked either confused or angry.

But not as angry as I was.

"Why didn't you let me go after him?" I asked.

From my side, Luana elbowed me hard in the ribs. "Shush."

I glared at her.

After the warlock escaped, after the less than stellar trained guards from Unity chased after him, and after the crowd dispersed and hid inside their homes, my mother guided me up the hill to her house. On the way, we found Luana, who was coming down to meet us.

"What happened?" she asked, immediately noticing the tension between us.

With an emotionless tone, my mother told Luana all that had occurred—the invasion, having the warlock secured, the magic stealing spell, the counter-attack, the warlock running away, the guards going after him.

Luana couldn't believe that had just happened. She offered to help in any way she could.

"Keeran has already done more than enough," was my mother's curt answer.

Anger lashed out of me, but before I could transfer it to her, I walked past her and entered my cabin. To my dismay, she followed Luana and me inside, and started working a hole in the floor with all her pacing.

Finally, my mother stopped pacing and turned her hard gaze to me. "Are you seriously asking why I wouldn't let you go after him?"

I shrugged. "I think I know what my freaking words mean."

Her hands balled into fists. I thought she would yell at me. Instead, she let out a long breath and relaxed her hands. "I guess I was expecting too much of you. I asked you to steal his magic when I knew you had barely attempted this spell before. It was my mistake." She paused. "And because of that, he got away."

"Your guards will find him," Luana said, her tone sympathetic.

Was she really siding with my mother right now?

"I don't think they will." A sob rose to her throat. "It's happening. My prophecy. It'll come to pass. This warlock will tell Isalia about Unity, and she will come to destroy it."

My rage spiked, turning my blood to fire and tainting my vision red.

"All you care about is this cursed place," I shouted. "It's all about keeping Unity safe. You love this place more than you love your own son."

"Keeran," Luana snapped.

"You know what?" I continued. "If you love it so much, then have it all to yourself. Marry it. Have a family with the town. Be happy. Because I don't freaking care anymore!" I brushed my hands down my arms, as if washing myself of her and her town.

"By the moon," Luana whispered.

"You too." I pointed a finger to Luana's face. "You love it here so much, you side with this witch all the time, why don't you stay here? I'm tired of this freaking game."

Luana's eyes were huge. "What the hell are you talking about? A game? What game?"

"It's the amulet," my mother said.

"No! It's not!" I screamed. How dare she say something about it? The amulet was the most powerful, the most *important* thing right now. With this amulet, with the power it carried, I would defeat Isalia and her she-wolves and her warlocks. I would clear Luana's throne, so she could take it, and I would become the most powerful warlock lord of all time. My magic flared inside me. "You two—"

Something hit my chest and robbed me of air. Suddenly dizzy, I fell seated on the couch behind me.

"What did you do?" Luana asked. She scurried to my side.

I blinked, trying to make sense of what was happening, of my surroundings.

"It's just a weak stunning spell," my mother said, as if that was the most normal thing. "He was losing it. I had to do something. Hopefully, he'll regain some clarity until the spell fades."

What I felt was the life and energy seeping out of me. Tendrils of power clung to me, tugging me down, but at this point, I couldn't make out what was real or what was a hallucination, a vision induced by the stunning spell.

"Just breathe." Luana cupped her hand on my cheek and whispered again, "In and out. Just breathe."

I didn't know how long I focused on her, following her lead with inhales and exhales. Finally, my heartbeat slowed, my magic and the magic of the amulet faded from my veins, and I realized they had been right. I had been vulnerable when attempting the magic stealing spell, then became irritated when the warlock fought back, and enraged when he had escaped—all bad feelings that allowed the amulet to send its dark magic into me.

"I'm sorry," I muttered.

Luana smoothed her hand down my cheek and neck. "It's okay. You're fine now."

I shook my head. "I'm not fine. The warlock escaped because of me."

Luana's eyes widened. "The mirror! We can find him with the mirror!" She dashed to the bedroom and came back with the mirror in her hands. "We found the mirror!" she announced to my mother.

"That's ... that's good," Acalla said, clearly disheartened.

"No, not good," Luana said. She pushed the mirror into Acalla's hands. "The mirror has a cool magic. We can use it to spy on anyone. Ask it to show you the warlock."

Acalla's brows curled down. "Show me the warlock."

I stood and came to their side. The mirror frosted over, then the surface swirled toward the center. It was like the frost and smoke were being swallowed by a hole in the middle. When the frost and smoke were gone, we saw it. The warlock ran through the forest, using his magic to speed his pace.

"Where is this?" Luana asked.

"I can't tell," Acalla said. "There are trees and bushes. Nothing I recognize." We watched it for a minute more. "I don't know where he is." She lowered the mirror. "I can only hope my guards find him."

She handed the mirror back to Luana and dragged her feet out of the cabin.

I plopped down on the couch again.

What the hell had I done?

11

LUANA

WYATT LEANED OVER THE LIST SITTING ON THE COFFEE TABLE. "Where else could we check?"

Seated beside him, Farrah shook her head, making her long silver hair sway back and forth. "I don't know."

A strong sense of déjà vu hit me every time Wyatt, Farrah, and I got together to research.

Once upon a time, Keeran, Drake, and I had spent hours, days, weeks reading hundreds of books, trying to find a way to save Thea from a horrible fate.

Now, I needed to find the other two items the Starlight wolves warned me about—the dagger of all hunting, and the crown of all branches.

A month had passed since the warlock had escaped from Unity, and despite everyone being on high alert, nothing had happened. I had tried using the mirror to look for him, but it wouldn't show him anymore. It was like the mirror could only show a person once, or it had to recharge.

Keeran had been quiet and reserved since then. He still blamed himself for letting the warlock escape and putting

Unity in danger. He hadn't mentioned it, but I knew he was also upset about his last outburst. It had been the amulet, not him, but it still messed with him.

Despite his feelings, he still met his mother for magic lesson. At least he wasn't sulking all day.

Meanwhile, Wyatt, Farrah, and I focused on finding the other two items. The dagger and the crown had to be somewhere, but where?

Wyatt moved the pen over the list. "We checked the surrounding area. The caves, the streams, the hills ... unless you have a better idea of where the dagger and the crown could be, I don't think we should waste time searching aimlessly."

"What about the books?" I asked. With Thea's curse, Drake had traveled the country, looking for libraries with hidden magical sections.

"We already searched Unity's library," Farrah said.

"And Almae's personal collection," Wyatt added. "And some of the residents' books too."

"We didn't find anything about these items, or magical werewolves, for that matter," Farrah said.

I looked at the list. Several places, books, knowledgeable people to ask. There wasn't much on our list, and I honestly had no idea where to look next. Like Wyatt said, we couldn't wander through the forest and hope to stumble on them. One, we weren't that lucky. Two, the items could be thousands of miles away.

We would never find them if we couldn't narrow down the search.

"We need more clues," I whispered.

"Can the dagger and the crown do anything special?" Wyatt asked. "I mean, like the mirror. It can be used to spy on someone. Do the other items have similar characteristics?"

A couple of days ago, I had met with Romulus and Meira again. I had begged them for more info on the remaining two items. Any clue as to where they could be, but they didn't know. But since I mentioned discovering what the mirror could do, they told me about one more.

"I have no idea what the crown does or looks like, but they told me the dagger is silver with a long hilt and the face and horns of a stag imprinted on the pummel."

Farrah sat straighter. "What does it do?"

"It can be used to mark an enemy for death," I said. "Once you use the dagger to mark someone for death, they have only a limited time until death finds them."

Farrah shot to her feet. "I know where that dagger is!"

I rose with her. "What? Where?"

"It's called something different in my realm, but I'm certain I've seen this dagger before in a fae fortress a couple of days southeast of here."

"Here? On Earth? Not in the fae realm?" That seemed too good to be true. "Are you sure?"

Farrah nodded vehemently. "Yes."

"H-how do we get there?"

"It's ... it won't be easy to get to it." Farrah frowned. "The fae who inhabit that fortress are different from my brother and me. They aren't frost fae."

Wyatt stood to face us. "You mean, they are your enemies."

She dipped her chin. "Yes, they are my enemies."

"No, don't say that!" Just a few seconds ago, the dagger had been within my grasp.

"Well, if you really need the dagger, I guess we can always try to break into the fortress and steal it," Farrah suggested.

"Break in? Steal it?" Wyatt shook his head. "Not sure I like that. We've been through a lot already."

"Nobody said gathering these items would be easy," I said. "If it were, then they wouldn't still be missing." I glanced at Farrah. "You have been to this fortress, right? Can you guide us there? Could you guide us inside?"

Like a soldier ready for battle, Farrah nodded. "Yes, I can."

Keeran walked into the cabin, his forehead dripping with sweat. Today's magic lesson must have been hard. "What can you do?" he asked.

"They are planning how to break into a fae fortress and steal the dagger of all hunting," Wyatt told him.

"Wait, what?" Keeran lifted a finger. "You found the dagger and it's inside a fortress?"

"And we plan on breaking in and stealing," Farrah said, not a hint of fear or worry in her voice.

"Back up a minute," Keeran said. "How do you know this is the dagger you're looking for?"

"Farrah said she's seen it before," I explained. "At this fortress."

Keeran shook his head. "Luana, remember the crystal cave? It was dangerous, and there were booby traps. Now you're talking about breaking into a fortress. That means it's heavily guarded."

His opposition grated on my nerves. Was the amulet acting up again? I really didn't know how much more patience I had for his outbursts.

"We can do it," Farrah said. "I've been there multiple times before. I know all the ins and outs. I'm sure we can do it."

"You're nuts for encouraging this," Keeran barked at her.

Farrah's bright blue eyes rounded.

Wyatt took a step forward. "Hey, don't talk to her like that."

The veins in Keeran's neck popped. "Like what? Like the three of you have gone crazy over Luana's little quest?"

"Crazy?" Farrah faced him. Despite being much shorter than him, she didn't seem one ounce intimidated by him. "You want to talk about crazy? Look in the mirror!"

"Why you—"

I grabbed Keeran's rising arm. "By the moon, what were you going to do? Attack Farrah?"

He glanced at his hand, his wrist secured in my grip, as if he had never seen it before. Was he so out of it that he hadn't even noticed he was about to throw his magic at Farrah?

Keeran blinked. "What the ...?" He jerked his arm free and stomped out of the cabin.

I hesitated, but then followed him out.

"If I were you, I would give him a few minutes," Wyatt said.

I turned around. "You saw how he is. He seemed confused about what just happened."

"I saw him and he's losing it." Wyatt approached me. "I know you want to help, we all do, but there isn't much we can do if he doesn't want help."

"Give him some time, Luana," Farrah said. "In his state, he might end up hurting you, and he'll regret that forever."

I knew they were right, but it hurt so much. I hated seeing Keeran like this. I hated not being able to do much. What could I do? Take the amulet from him. But if I did that, the magic would be broken, and Soren would be able to escape the amulet.

The other option was the magic stealing spell, but that one had already caused too much trouble. Besides, Almae mentioned that Keeran was afraid of trying it again.

After I found the dagger and the crown, after I became the alpha of the Starlight pack, after we took down Isalia and brought peace to our corner of the world, I would focus on helping Keeran. There had to be another way, and I would find it.

"All right." Determined, I picked up a map from the coffee table. "Let's plan how to break into the fortress."

12

My hands shook as I paced the clearing.

After almost attacking Farrah, I had bolted from the cabin and ran to the first place that popped in my mind—the clearing I trained with my mother. Since our lesson for the day was over, I knew it would be deserted, and I wouldn't hurt anyone here.

I halted in the center and glanced at my hands.

What the hell had I almost done? I was losing control and I couldn't even explain it. I couldn't make sense of it.

I slid my hand to my chest, to where the amulet rested against my skin underneath my shirt. Luana and my mother kept saying the amulet was doing this to me, but it couldn't be. The amulet was good. It was powerful. It would make me invincible. It would help us win against Isalia. It would make Luana the strongest alpha, and I would be the most powerful warlock lord.

"Keeran."

I spun around, my hands raised, ready to defend myself. Or to attack.

Upon seeing my mother standing at the edge of the clearing, I lowered my arms. "What do you want?"

With her gentle eyes locked on mine, my mother walked toward me. "Why don't you walk a little with me?"

I frowned at her. "I'm good."

She hooked her arm through mine and tugged. "Indulge an old lady, will you?"

I groaned, but let her take me into the forest. In silence, she led us down a narrow path that flanked Unity's border. Acalla kept a small floating orb of light beside us to drive away the darkness. The chilly night air filled my lungs, but didn't do much to clear my head or ease my tension.

Finally, she broke the silence. "Soren wasn't always evil, you know. He was a warlock with a good heart and good intentions. But power corrupts even the purest of hearts. Power and dark magic changed him."

I frowned, not expecting this topic. "Did you ever love him?"

"It was a complicated relationship," she said, her voice low. "When I met him, he was already consumed by power, but I could see glimpses of the man he used to be. It was hard to resist him when he treated me so well."

"Do you think he loved you?"

She nodded. "In his own twisted way, yes. I think so."

"Why didn't you fight for him? Why didn't you help him?"

"I was a single witch against the most powerful warlock in existence. There wasn't much I could do." She paused. "But the truth is, he didn't want to change. He loved the power and the magic. He loved being in control of everything and everyone."

"Then, why didn't you leave him sooner?"

"I was planning to, but then he gave me you." She turned

a soft smile at me. "I couldn't bear the thought of running away with you and you growing up fatherless." She let out a long breath. "Not that it helped much. You ended up growing up without both parents."

"Because you had the prophecy?"

She nodded. "Because of the prophecy."

"If you knew it was bad, why did you tell him?"

"I didn't have a choice," she whispered.

"What do you mean?"

"I vowed never to tell him, but he tortured me." Tears brimmed in her eyes. "I tried resisting, I tried enduring, but I couldn't. I told him everything." She wiped at her eyes. "That's why I ran with you, and that's why I hid you from him."

My gut curled with rage and hurt. "Just more evidence that Soren was really evil."

"True," my mother said. "An evil like that has to be stopped at all costs."

I patted the amulet on my chest. "He's taken care of."

"Keeran." My mother halted. "I'm really sorry, but I must do this."

"What—?"

Darkness surrounded me. I swam in a black sea, the waves several feet tall, taking me down.

A moment later, I drowned.

First thing I felt was the cool grass beneath me. A little disoriented, I sat up and looked around the clearing.

What the hell had happened?

I shot to my feet, and it hit me like an avalanche. My

mother had done something to me. She had put me to sleep, and now, she was nowhere to be seen. But why?

Instinctively, my hand flew to my chest.

The amulet was gone.

My mother had taken the amulet from me.

Angry, I cast a tracking spell. But she was too good for me. She had blocked her location from me. If I had to go after her the old-fashioned way, so be it.

I started after her, intend on scouring the forest until I found her. Until I got the amulet back from her.

"Keeran!"

Hands raised and already casting a bolt, I turned toward the voice.

Farrah brought her hands up. "Hey, it's us."

I stared at Farrah and Wyatt ... and Luana. I knew them. I knew them well. They were my friends, and one of them was my mate. My freaking, beloved mate, and I still couldn't lower my arms.

"Keeran, it's okay." Luana stepped closer, her eyes on mine. "It's just us."

"W-what are you doing here?" I asked through gritted teeth. I turned the bolt into a small flame over my palm, bringing some light to the forest. But still, the magic inside me demanded release.

"We were worried about you," my mate said. "You were gone for a long time, I wanted to check if you're all right."

"He's not all right," Farrah muttered.

Luana halted right in front of me. "Keeran, focus on me." She reached for my hands—the flame floated in the air—and cradled them in hers. "Tell me what happened?"

The fury flared up again. "My mother! She cast a sleeping spell on me."

"Wait." Luana shook her head. "Why?"

I ripped my hands free and grasped at the place where the amulet should have been. "She took it. The amulet. She stole it from me. I have to find it."

"She must have a good—"

"I don't care!" I yelled. Luana flinched. "I don't care if she had a reason or not. I need to find her. I need to get the amulet back."

"We'll help you," Wyatt said.

I stared at him over Luana's shoulder.

"Yes, we'll help you," Farrah affirmed. "Do you have any idea where she went?"

I shook my head. "I was under her spell when she fled, and she's blocking my tracking spell."

"That's okay," Luana said, her voice too calm. "We can still look for her. She can't be far."

A couple of hours ago, they had been chastising me about the amulet, and now they would help me? That didn't make sense.

"What if we separate?" Farrah suggested. "Wyatt and I will go in one direction, and you two go in the other. Then, we'll circle around and meet each other."

"I like that," Luana said. "And whoever finds Almae first can call the others."

"Sounds good," Wyatt said.

Luana glanced at me. "Does that work for you?"

I stared between them all, the urge to yell at them too great. "Yes," I rasped.

After a short nod, Wyatt and Farrah took off.

Luana beckoned me follow her. "Come on." She disappeared into the forest.

I inhaled deeply, taming my magic before it exploded and

burnt down the trees and followed Luana. Thankfully, my mother hadn't blocked her scent, and Luana easily followed her trail.

We found my mother kneeling in the bed of a stream, the amulet in front of her, and a big rock in her hands.

She let the rock drop and smash the amulet.

"No!" I waved my hand and a burst of magic flew in her direction. It knocked her into the stream.

"Keeran!" Luana took off after my mother.

I took off after the amulet.

I pushed the rock away, and miraculously, found the amulet intact. I picked it up and swung the chain around my neck. Instantly, I felt its magic reaching into me, filling my veins, satiating my thirst as if I had spent days in the desert.

My rage renewed, I glared at my mother as Luana helped her up. "What the hell do you think you were doing?"

"I was only doing what's right, Keeran," she said, a sob cutting off her words. "I was trying to destroy the amulet before it destroys you." Another sob rocked her body. "But I failed. I tried magic, fire, and breaking it anyway I could think of, but it didn't work. The magic inside it is too great."

"You tricked me," I spat. "You betrayed me. You took something precious from me and tried to destroy it."

"Keeran, your mother is only trying to help," Luana said. "That amulet is poisoning you."

"It's for the best, my son," my mother whispered. "Please, give it to me. I'll get rid of it for you."

"I don't want to get rid of it," I barked.

"Keeran, please." My mother reached for me. "You're blind. Let us be your eyes. We want that amulet gone."

"Is that what you all want?" My body shook with rage.

"You want the amulet gone? Fine." I took a step back. "Consider it gone."

I spun on my heels and ran.

"Keeran!" Luana screamed.

I only ran faster.

"KEERAN, WAIT!" I SHOUTED.

Almae held my hand. "He's not in his right mind. Go after him."

She looked fragile, though. I couldn't just leave her here. "What about you?"

"I'll take care of her." Farrah stepped forward, taking my place and holding Almae's hand. "Just go."

I nodded and shifted, my clothes ripping into pieces. I would be faster in my wolf form. I started to run but paused. The crystal rose had fallen beside my torn clothes. I knew, if I left it there, Wyatt or Farrah would pick it up for me, but for some reason, I felt like I had to bring it with me.

I picked it up with my mouth, held it between my teeth, and ran.

I tried following Keeran's scent, but either the forest was confusing me or Keeran had thrown a spell to spread his scent everywhere, making it difficult for me to follow him.

I wouldn't give up that easily, though. I kept running, trying to be faster than him, thinking where I would go if I were him. But this place was strange to us. We didn't have anything or know anyone nearby. He would probably simply march in a straight line until he was far from here.

Besides, it was late, already too dark. My eyes adjusted to the darkness just fine, but still it wasn't the same as running through the forest in the middle of the day.

Desperation filled every inch of my body as the time passed and I didn't seem any closer to him. Frantic, I stopped and used another technique.

The crystal rose.

Aren't you pure magic? Help me out. Lead me to my mate.

Instantly, the rose glowed its warm, red light, and a tug started in my chest. It pulled me forward, showing me the way.

Tears brimmed in my eyes.

Thank you.

Without a second to waste, I raced forward, letting the rose's magic lead me.

I ran for another two miles, until the tug stopped and the rose's glow was gone.

Holding my breath, I stepped past some bushes, and found a small lake nestled between two big rock formations. His hair messed up and his face ragged, Keeran stood at the water's edge. His hand was pressed against his chest, covering the amulet that once again hung from his neck.

I shifted back to my human form. "Keeran."

He turned dark eyes toward me. "What are you doing here?"

"I came to talk to you." I slowly approached him, afraid he would attack me. Keeran wasn't himself. "Ask you to come home with me."

He snorted. "Home. Unity was never our home."

"You're right, it's not. But it's where we're staying right now." I beckoned him to come to me. "Please, come back with me."

"Why? So Acalla can spell me again and take the amulet? So I can be reminded that she loves Unity more than she ever love me?" He shook his head. "No, thank you. I'm on my own now."

I reached for him and rested my hand on his arm. "You're not alone. No matter what happens, I'm with you."

He rolled his arm, making me drop my hand. "No, you're not. You side with Acalla. You're just saying that so I'll go back with you." He leaned closer and said through gritted teeth, "I won't."

"Okay, you won't." I would indulge him, just keep him talking. Relaxing. Although, I wasn't anywhere near relaxed. I rarely minded being naked, but being naked while arguing with my mate? I was too self-conscious. "What will you do, then?"

He looked out at the lake, barely visibly under the cloudy sky. "I will kill Isalia, release her wolves, and claim my warlocks. I'll become the warlock lord again."

I shook my head. "You never cared about being the warlock lord before. Why now?"

He snapped his head at me as if I had slapped him. "I never cared about being the warlock lord? Of course I did. I had doubts, yes, but it wasn't as if I didn't want it. I always did. I still do." He glanced down at his closed fists. "I am the warlock lord."

"Keeran, you don't need to do this alone. We're in this together." Never mind that he knew I wanted to take down Isalia myself. I wouldn't argue about that right now. "We're—"

"We're nothing."

I stared at him. "What?"

His eyes were cold. Harsh. Dark. "Fate might be having a laugh over making us mates, but I don't love you. I don't want you." He touched the amulet again, his fingers caressing it like a lover. "Not anymore."

A gasp rose from my throat, and my heart shriveled in my chest. "You can't be serious."

A wicked grin fell on his lips. "I am. You're just a filthy dog who is pretending she's some powerful creature with magic. That's a fairy tale, and let me tell you something, fairy tales are just make believe. They don't exist."

Tears burning my eyes, I took a step back. "You're breaking up with me."

He nodded. "I should never have started anything with you. Glad I came to my senses sooner rather than later."

I stared at him, waiting for him to laugh and tell me it was a joke. But he didn't. Keeran was so consumed by the amulet's darkness that he really believed this crap. He believed he was better off alone. He believed he could take on Isalia and her army alone. He believed he didn't care about his mother.

He believed he didn't love me anymore.

On instinct, I swiped at the amulet, but Keeran was faster. He leaned back just out of reach. I went for it again, but he raised a shield between us. I hit the shield and fell on my ass.

"Come at me again and I'll burn you alive." Flames appeared in his hands.

He was serious. He was downright serious.

Holding on to my pride, I stood. I was done here. I wouldn't beg; I wouldn't cry. I tried taking the amulet from him, but he was ready to kill me if I did.

Keeran was gone, and I could do nothing to bring him back.

I puffed my chest and lifted my chin. "I hope you realize what you're doing ... and don't die regretting it. Goodbye, Keeran."

Without looking back, I shifted into a wolf, grabbed the crystal rose from the ground, and ran.

Keeran had made his choice. I wouldn't think of him; I wouldn't cry for him. I would find the remaining two items and make Isalia pay.

14

KEERAN

Luana left.

She just left.

I stared at the trees where she had just run by and disappeared, my rage warring inside of me against other feelings.

Feelings I couldn't name. Feelings I had forgotten.

Numb, I looked down at the amulet.

It was the most precious thing in my life.

Right?

I took it off and stared at it, confused. I need it so much, it hurt. But why? Why did I feel like I would die without it?

The magic inside the amulet stirred. It brushed against my palm, caressing me. It seeped into my skin, and tangled with my bones and muscles. It advanced inch by inch, claiming the air, the water, the blood inside me.

And I let it.

I let the magic claim me.

Because it felt good. Because it made me powerful. Strong. Unstoppable.

Dark.

Evil.

Crazy.

I threw the amulet on the ground and stepped back.

They were right. My mother and Luana had been right. The dark magic inside the amulet, my father's dark magic, was poisoning me, robbing me of my thoughts and controlling my actions.

I had insulted my mother, snapped at Farrah and Wyatt, and said awful things to Luana. I let her walk out of my life as if she didn't matter. When in truth, she was the only thing that mattered. She was my mate, the love of my life, and I had been so blind, so drunk, so soaked in dark magic, I had no control in what I did or didn't do.

I had let the cursed amulet consume me, feeding me illusions about being a warlock lord and having infinite power.

I confess I had wanted the title. I had wavered at first, confused about what it meant. I had even told Zell that I would gladly pass the title to someone else, so I wouldn't become evil. I would have if it had come to that, but that didn't mean I would be happy about it, that it was what I wanted.

For someone who didn't have any direction in life for so long, suddenly finding out I could be more ... it was dazzling. Alluring. The dark magic in the amulet knew that was one of my weakness. It fed on it. It thrived.

It poisoned me.

No more.

I wouldn't let it poison and use me.

I channeled my power, filling my veins with my magic. This freaking game was over. It was never my intention to kill my father, but if I needed to destroy this amulet to recover my mind, to recover my life, I would.

Even before I attacked it, the amulet started shaking, as if erupting from the inside.

I barely had time to react, as a dark shadow burst from the amulet. The shadow twirled once, twice, then shaped into a human silhouette.

Jaw open, I watched as Soren took shape—his long hair loose, his robes in tatters, but his back straight and his chin high. Despite looking like before, he wasn't whole. His skin shimmered black, as if he were made of shadow and smoke, and his eyes had a gray hue to them.

Somehow, Soren found enough power to project a shadow of himself outside the amulet.

"My son," he started, his voice hoarse, as if it hadn't been used in a long time. "You thought it would be that easy to get rid of me?"

I forced my mouth closed. "This isn't you."

"Of course, this is me." He gestured to his ghostlike body. "You made me like this."

"I ..."

He walked toward me. "Keeran ..."

I retreated and raised my hand. "Stay back." In the shock of seeing him escaping the amulet, I had let go of my magic, but I grasped for it.

Soren stopped. "I've seen what they did to you, Keeran."

I frowned. "Who?"

"Your mother and your mate. Those women aren't on your side, my son." He shook his head, his face shimmering. "They want your power; they want my power. You can't let them have it." His shadow hovered closer to me. "You have to destroy them. You have to kill them."

"No," I whispered.

"They don't deserve you. No one deserves you," he went

on. "You're like me. Powerful, strong, unbreakable. You can reign over the world. You can be the warlock lord you always wanted to be."

I stared at the shadow, shocked by his words. My father wouldn't say any of that to me. He wanted to be the most powerful warlock lord ever born. He would rather die than let me have the title.

No, this wasn't Soren's shadow.

It was the dark magic.

The dark magic had created an illusion, and despite not having the amulet with me right now, it was still trying to manipulate me, to use me. To consume me.

The dark magic had done it all. It had seeped into my mind, it had altered my thoughts and feelings, and it had made me angry and nasty and just plain vicious.

Evil.

I had been evil.

I gasped as if a blow had been dealt to my gut. I had pushed everyone away. I had been horrible to Luana. I had told her things I never meant.

I don't love you. I don't want you.

That had been the darkness talking, not me. I still loved and wanted Luana, and always would.

"Put the amulet back on," the shadow said. "Put it back on and let me help you. Let's kill them together. Let's kill them all."

As if my head was clear for the first time in months, I realized what I had to do.

I called my power and focused.

Then, I released Soren from the amulet.

The shadow faded into the air, as Soren, flesh and blood and still full of darkness, appeared in front of me. His black, bleak eyes looked around, lost. His frame swayed, too weak. The darkness had played on him too, feeding on him while it manipulated me.

We both had been controlled and abused by it.

No more.

Soren blinked, his gaze finally fixing on me. "Keeran?" he asked, his voice hoarse from lack of use.

For a moment, I felt like a coward. He had no way of fighting me, and yet, if I didn't do it now, I would never do it.

"I'm sorry," I whispered.

I sent my magic toward my father. I pushed it inside him. As quickly as I could, I searched for the source.

Soren's eyes widened. "Keeran, what are you doing?"

Unlike other warlocks, Soren had many little sources hidden within himself. I searched and grabbed for them one by one. When I was sure there was nothing left inside him, I pulled.

"No!" Soren rasped as he opened his hands and called his power. He tried channeling it, commanding it, but he was too weak to hold it. "That's mine! It's my magic!"

"I know, but I can't let you have it." I closed my fists and tugged.

Despite his weakened state, Soren put up a fight. He resisted, he gritted his teeth, he tried to take the magic and throw it like a weapon at me. But it didn't work. Right now, I had the upper hand.

Right now, I was winning.

With one last effort, I pulled and the magic soared from him.

Soren's eyes glazed over, his skin grew gray, his mouth fell open, and his body became flaccid.

His magic floated toward me, a long dark snake swirling

around a much thinner, much smaller red trail. The darkness covering his real magic. Not wanting to be tainted by the black magic, I closed my hands, as if grabbing the two magics by the tail, and opened my arms wide, pulling them apart. The dark snake fought me, trying to hold on to the red one, but I was in control now. It couldn't resist me.

Then, I opened my hand and let it go. The rest of the dark magic, the evilness, faded like smoke in the night air, while the red seeped into me. I had successfully absorbed my father's magic.

"It's done," I whispered to myself. "I won."

Despite the new boost in my power, I didn't feel victorious. I felt like crap. After imprisoning him inside an amulet, I had stolen his magic and made my father into the catatonic figure standing in front of me.

His memories flashed in my mind, giving me a headache. Groaning, I bucked forward, fighting it. I bet my mother didn't know about this side effect.

I inhaled deeply, trying to control my thoughts, slow them down. Damn it, this would take time to get used to.

The one good thing of all of this was that the amulet and the darkness were gone. Now, I had a long road to follow. I would beg Luana and the others for forgiveness.

I just hoped they were willing to listen to me. Shit, I hoped they allowed me back into Unity.

Determined to make up with them any way I could, I grasped my father's shoulders, and dragged his barely walking body back to Unity.

15

LUANA

GLISTENING UNDER THE SETTING SUN, THE DARK GRAY FORTRESS was like a sore thumb against the green mountain. Despite that, it was impressive with tall towers, round balconies, and dark vines entwined across the stone, looking like part of the supporting structure.

"It's beautiful," I said.

Farrah turned her bright blue eyes to me. "You mean, in an eerie, creepy way, right?"

I shrugged. "I wasn't going to say it …"

"But it is." She returned her gaze to the fortress in the distance. "The dagger will be on the first floor, in an area with several artifacts and other valuables." She pulled her silver hair up and tied it into a ponytail, revealing her slightly pointed ears. "The inside of the fortress isn't heavily guarded, but the outside is. If we want to avoid fighting, we'll have to find a way to sneak inside."

I frowned. "You said you knew this place well."

"I do," she muttered. I wondered why, but once more didn't press her for answers. "I have a plan for that."

"And once inside?" Wyatt asked. He had been quiet for the most part of our journey. Now, though, he seemed ready for anything.

"We need to avoid patrols, but other than that, it should be easy."

"What about the prince?" I asked. Farrah had told us a fae prince reigned over the fortress.

"He'll probably be in the main hall, pretending he's still at his court, commanding his subjects," she said. From the tone of her voice, I gathered she didn't like this prince much.

"You said he isn't a frost fae, right?" Wyatt asked.

"No." Farrah shook her head. "He's much worse."

I didn't like the sound of that, but she didn't give me time to ask more as she trudged forward, and Wyatt and I had to scramble to follow her.

We had been on the road since the day before, traveling from Unity. We had used our usual tactic: walk to the nearest road, steal a car, and take it as far as it could take us. Then, we abandoned it on the side of the road, and entered the forest again. We had to come up with a better way of traveling. Wasn't Almae a powerful witch? Couldn't she conjure portals for us? Or teleport us? That would certainly save time.

As we hiked up the mountain, careful with possible patrols and traps, my mind took off—again. I had tried keeping myself busy ever since I walked away from Keeran yesterday. Wyatt, Farrah, and I had embarked on this crazy mission of stealing the dagger from the fae prince, but my thoughts of Keeran overshadowed everything else. Every time I had a second to breathe, he was back in the front row.

It hurt. Breaking up with Keeran, having to walk away from him ... it hurt more than a thousand strikes and bites.

Unfortunately, the world wouldn't stop so I could nurse

my heartbreak. Isalia's threat still hung over our heads, she still had control over wolves and warlocks, and she would come for us soon.

We had to be ready.

I had to be ready. I had to find the next two items. I had to recover my magic, get my pack together and defeat her.

Yet, with each step I took toward the fae fortress, a pang cut through my heart, reminding me of what I was leaving behind. Of who I had left behind.

It didn't matter. It had been Keeran's choice. He was the one who embraced the darkness and left us.

Left me.

Boots crunched dried grass. On instinct, I grabbed Farrah's and Wyatt's arms and halted.

Wyatt glanced at me, probably picking it up with his enhanced hearing.

"Patrol?" Farrah mouthed.

I nodded.

We crouched behind some bushes and waited. Not a minute later, four fae dressed in elaborated black and silver armor and carrying long spears with shimmering blades marched past us.

I waited until their footsteps faded with the rest of the mountain's sounds. "What now?"

Farrah offered me a knowing grin. "Now we break in."

"How?" Wyatt asked.

"Come with me." Farrah stood and walked three steps forward. Once Wyatt and I were beside her, she swirled her hands in front of her body, invoking her magic.

I felt the chill of the ice enveloping me, rising from my toes to my head. "What are you doing?"

"Glamouring us," she said simply. "This isn't my specialty, though, so I can't hold it for long. Let's get this over with."

She stomped ahead.

I looked down at myself. She glamoured us? Into what? Besides the feeling of her cold magic against my skin, I didn't see anything.

"Look." Wyatt elbowed me.

My heart skipped a beat as I witnessed Farrah walking straight to the front gate, where two fae warriors stood guard.

The warriors saw her coming and straightened.

"What are you doing here?" one asked, his tone sharp.

Farrah stood tall. One of her hands was lifted midair beside her, as if she was holding something. I narrowed my eyes.

The spear. She was pretending to hold a spear.

We were glamoured to look like the warriors.

I tugged on Wyatt's arms and rushed to Farrah's side.

"Your shift isn't over," the second warrior said. He had a nasty scar cutting through his thick, dark eyebrow.

"It is for this evening," she said, her voice firm. I couldn't hear it, but I bet she had changed that too. "The other team is ready to come out." She gestured toward the gates. "You can go ahead and confirm. I'm sure General Auron will be glad to be asked about the patrols routes and times again."

The two warriors exchanged a concerned glance. With a heavy sigh, they stepped aside, and pressed their hands to a darker spot on the gray stone wall. Dark smoke surged from the ground as the black gate rose.

She grunted, as if that was enough thanks, and walked in.

Holding my breath, I followed her, with Wyatt at my side.

Farrah didn't miss a beat as she crossed the courtyard.

She only hesitated when she glanced at the main entrance, then she hurried her steps and rounded a corner to the left.

There, she led us to a door of frosted glass and into a long corridor.

I couldn't help but wonder how she knew this place. How she knew the fae prince, and why she hadn't chosen a more diplomatic way of asking for the dagger instead of sneaking into a heavily guarded fortress.

Although, she had mentioned they were from enemy courts. But if it was that bad, she would have said something, wouldn't she?

Faint footsteps filled my ears. "Someone is coming," I muttered.

Farrah waved toward a door to our right. We stepped into the dark room. Careful, we spied out. A female fae, with long dark hair pulled into a tight bun at her nape, and wearing a long but simple black dress, crossed the corridor. She had a glass tray in her hands.

"Time for a new disguise," Farrah said.

Her magic tickled against my skin, and I could only imagine she had changed us from warriors to maids.

Wyatt grunted. "Am I wearing a dress?"

Farrah smiled. "You're a cute female fae."

He rolled his eyes.

I focused my hearing, but the sounds were distant. "I think this is our chance."

Farrah took the lead. Trying to walk meekly like the maid we had seen, Farrah guided us down the corridor, past a tall staircase, across a grand foyer with light gray stones on the floor and a dark crystal chandelier. Then, we entered another hallway, and Farrah crossed under a large archway.

"Here we are," she said.

The place reminded me of one of the rooms in DuMoir Castle, where art, paintings, and other priceless artifacts were stored. However, this place was more like a long and wide corridor with several paintings and some sculptures along the walls.

"Where's the dagger?" I asked, looking around.

"Here." Farrah sprinted to the middle of the long corridor, then pointed to the wall on the right.

The dagger—a beautiful weapon with a long, white hilt, and a curved, dark blade—rested against the wall.

I gasped. "This is the dagger of all hunting? Are you sure?"

"I am," Farrah said.

Hands ready, I advanced on it. But before my fingers could touch it, an energy ricocheted toward me. Yelping with the sting, I retreated a few steps. "It's protected."

"Of course he would do that." Farrah groaned. "Let me try."

Farrah channeled her magic. The air around us cooled. Ice crawled up the wall toward the dagger, but it didn't reach it. The ice kept taking over the wall, toward the ceiling, but a large circle was left intact around the dagger, as if its magic or the protection around it was a strong shield and kept the ice away.

Hands raised, and fingers shaped like a claw, Farrah groaned and pushed more of her magic against the shield. A dome of ice formed around the dagger, and still, Farrah couldn't reach it.

She grounded her feet into the floor and yelled. More of her magic flew out and pushed against the dagger's protection.

Cracks appeared in the ice.

Then it exploded, sending several icicles flying toward us. I raised both my hands, protecting my face, but some of the icicles grazed my arms.

When I lowered my hands, Farrah was on her knees, breathing hard and sweat beading her forehead.

Hand bleeding from one of the flying icicles, Wyatt reach for her. "Are you okay?"

She nodded. "I'm okay. I'll be fine." She tipped her chin at me. "It should be fine now. Go get it."

I hesitated for a moment.

My heart raced as I lunged at the wall and caught the dagger effortlessly from its hooks. It was light as a plume, and its magic tingled my skin. I gripped it tight, suddenly eager and relieved, as if I had accomplished the hardest of all the tasks.

As if I was one step closer to my destiny.

I grinned at Farrah. "Thank you."

Holding on to Wyatt, Farrah stood and shook her head. "Don't thank me yet. We still have to get out of here."

Wyatt and I froze as the sound echoed in our ears.

Footsteps advanced our way.

"We have to hurry," I urged.

Wyatt glanced around. "There's no other exit."

Farrah frowned. "What's going on?"

The footsteps grew closer.

"There's no time," I whispered.

"Shit," Wyatt muttered as over a dozen fae warriors swarmed into the room.

They surrounded us and pointed their shimmering blades at our chests.

I didn't think and I simply started shifting.

Farrah grabbed my arm. "Don't bother," she whispered,

just for our wolf ears. "There are fourteen here, but there are way more outside this room. But these kind of fae are powerful. We can't fight them all and win."

What was she suggesting? That we give up? Surrender, just like that?

And what did she mean by these kind of fae? She had said they were enemies, so probably different courts, but which one? They were different from her. They eyes were several shades of brown, their skin was darker, and their hair was pitch black. But other than appearance, I had no idea what she meant.

A tall male fae stepped out from the bunch of warriors, his movement sharp and defined. His armor was different, with pointier pauldrons, and details in silver. Instead of carrying a spear like the others, he had a long sword hanging from his hip.

He halted in front of us and stared at Farrah. Contradicting everything I expected of him, the fae's mouth curled into a smile. "Welcome, Lady Farrah."

16

IT WAS LATE WHEN I RETURNED TO UNITY AND MADE MY WAY toward the cabin Luana and I shared. I wondered if she would let me in.

Dreading confronting her and being rejected, I tugged on Soren's arm and veered to my mother's house—like a freaking coward. Lights shone through the window panels, which meant she was home and awake.

I stopped before the door and glanced at my zombie father. How would she react if she saw him like that? It would be better if I prepared her first, so I pushed my father to the side of the door, under the shadows, where she wouldn't see him if she didn't step out.

Taking a deep breath, I knocked on the door.

The door flew open a moment later, and my mother stared at me with disbelief written all over her face. "Keeran? But ... how?" She took a step back, as if I could be an illusion, a ghost who came back to haunt her. "Luana went to find you. Then, she came back crying, saying you were gone, that you weren't coming back."

A sigh escaped my lips. "I have so much to apologize for."

My mother narrowed her eyes. "What ... are you okay? Keeran, are you back?"

I nodded. "I'm me again, Mother. No more evil or darkness within me."

She let out a relieved cry and wrapped her arms around my shoulders and held me tight. "I'm so glad you're back, Keeran." She suddenly pulled back and glanced to my neck. "But ... where's the necklace? What happened?"

I shrugged. "I have no idea where the necklace is. All I can say is that it's useless now." I reached to the side and took hold of Soren's arm. I pulled him, until he was standing right beside me. "He escaped the amulet and I stole his magic."

A hand covering her open mouth, my mother stared at Soren, the man she once loved. I couldn't imagine how hard it was for her to see him like that. A shell of a man, a zombie, a walking corpse. If it made me disgusted with myself and sad, I only wondered how she felt.

My mother reached over to Soren and placed a shaking hand on his face. "Oh, Soren. I'm so sorry. I'm so sorry for everything." A sob rose up her throat. "If only you hadn't gone so deep into the dark, if only you didn't let the evil overtake you ..." She retreated a step and took a deep breath, cutting the tears short before they even started. "It had to be done. In a way, you saved him, Keeran. And now you're free of his darkness. In the end, that's all the matters."

I knew that. I knew it had to be done, that I had to win somehow, but it still made me feel sad. I didn't love my father —I had barely known him—but he was still my freaking father. It hurt just the same.

"What are we going to do with him now?" I asked.

My mother snapped her fingers and a white spark

exploded from them. The spark floated around me and traveled down the hill. "The healer will come to take him in a minute."

"The healer? You think he can be saved from this state?"

She shook her head. "No. This is permanent, but I never met someone affected by this spell before. Since he's still living, we should make sure he's all right, health wise. The healer will let us know if something isn't right." She stared at Soren for a second. "Then we'll find him a home and take care of him."

"I'm here," the healer said from behind me. Had she just appeared there? Could she do that? "What's the matter?"

My mother explained to the witch healer who the zombie-man was, what had happened, and what she should do with him. After nodding in agreement, the healer placed her hand under my father's arms and steered him away.

My mother offered me a forced smile. "You must be hungry. Come in. I'll make you something to eat."

I shook my head. "It's late, and I would rather talk to Luana now. The sooner I start to beg, the sooner she'll take me back."

My mother's face fell. "Oh."

I stilled. "What happened?"

"Luana left a few hours ago," my mother said. "She went with Wyatt and Farrah to find the dagger."

"Shit," I muttered. "Do you have any idea where they went?"

My mother tilted her head. "Keeran, Luana was really upset. She was devastated, actually. Going on this mission was her way of dealing with it. If you go after her, you'll probably only upset her. That might endanger the mission."

Damn it. I hadn't thought about that. My mother was

right, of course. I didn't know their plan; I could put everyone at risk, which would make Luana hate me more.

But staying here and waiting would be hard. I hated knowing she was out there, going on a dangerous mission without me. Farrah and Wyatt were strong, and I knew they would keep Luana safe, but my heart didn't want to quiet down so easily.

"I don't feel good about letting her go like that," I muttered.

"Keeran, this place they are going, it's a day from here," my mother said. "You'll never catch up with them."

"What do I do, then?" I asked, feeling like a lost puppy.

"Come in and dine with me." My mother stepped back, giving me space to enter her house. "We have a lot to talk about."

We sure did. I had to apologize again for being such a jerk. The darkness from the amulet had been affecting me before we came to Unity, and I was already angry and confused and practically gone when I met her. I had been a jackass from the start.

Moreover, now I was the real warlock lord and we had to talk strategy. Now, I could command the warlocks and order them to abandon Isalia and join my side—but that was only a theory. Most of them would probably sneer at me and remain by Isalia's side.

Besides, I needed to pass the time somehow. Staying alone in my cabin while Luana was gone would only make me more agitated and worried.

"Okay," I muttered before walking past the front door. "But you better make me something delicious."

My mother smiled at me. "It'll be divine."

17

THE FAE MALE AND THE FOURTEEN WARRIORS ESCORTED US INTO the main hall. Dark smooth stone covered the floors, white almost silver pillars adorned the naked walls, curving several feet above our heads, and meeting at the center, where dark crystal chandeliers hung. At the end of the room, a dais of black stone covered the space, and a black throne sat alone. Shadows shimmered behind the throne—I wondered if it was an illusion or a magic trick.

The fae prince sat on the throne, with one leg over the thick armrest, and his head thrown back. The moment we entered, he straightened and a huge smile took over his face.

Long black hair, smooth dark skin, thick eyebrows, and sharp angles, he had quite a beautiful face. The black crown on top of his head and the black suit with thick cloak embroidered with silver details, added to his character. When he stood, I realized he was tall. Despite that, he looked young. But I had to be wary. Fae didn't age like we did.

"Welcome to the Shade Fortress," he said, opening his arms. "This is quite the surprise."

We were escorted until we stood ten feet from the dais. Then, the warriors spread out, forming a semicircle around us, their spears pointed at us.

"I've caught them stealing this," the fae who escorted us here said. He gestured to the dagger of all hunting, resting in his hands.

"Thank you, General Auron." The fae prince turned his grin back to us. "Dear Lady Farrah, why don't you introduce your friends?"

Farrah stilled. I could hear her rapid heartbeat and her elaborated breathing. She didn't like this guy, but she didn't let it show.

Instead, she bowed her head to him and relaxed her shoulders. "These are my friends, werewolves Luana and Wyatt." She glanced at me, then Wyatt. "This is Prince Lark of the Court of Shadows."

"A fae friends with two werewolves," the prince mused. "I would like to hear how that happened."

"We don't have time for that," Farrah said, her tone polite. Careful. "We are on an important quest. That dagger is part of that quest. I would love it if you gave it to us."

The prince tilted his head, as if trying to read Farrah's mind. She stared at him, her heart going a million miles per hour, but her face didn't betraying her nervousness.

Since this was my quest, I cleared my throat and said, "Prince Lark, I'm the rightful heir of the Starlight pack. Long ago, my pack was attacked by an evil she-wolf. She killed my parents and destroyed everything. Recently, I found the remaining Starlight wolves, but I can't become their alpha if I don't get back my magic." At the same time, I wondered why I was being so honest, I tried reminding myself he was a ruler, a leader, just like I was supposed to be. Perhaps my tale would spark some sense of sympathy in him, and he would let us take the dagger without any trouble. "To get my magic back, I need three items. One of them is the dagger of all hunting." I pointed to the weapon in General Auron's hand. "This dagger."

"The Starlight pack," the prince said. He tipped his chin once. "I remember that pack. I stole this dagger from them, many, many years ago. It's a powerful item."

"I know," I said.

"So you must know I won't give it up," he said. His fake smile faded, and his eyes darkened. "Ask my people." He opened his arms, gesturing to the warriors in the main hall. "I'm not the most merciful ruler, but I am just. Why would I give the dagger to a filthy werewolf? Do you have anything valuable to trade for the dagger?"

"W-what?" I stared at him, lost. I hadn't expected this.

First, I hadn't expected being caught at all. Despite being a foolish plan, I had hoped to sneak in, steal the dagger, and sneak out. But when had our plans ever been so simple?

"Well?" the prince pressed.

I raked my brain, trying to think of something valuable I could give up. But there was nothing. I barely had crappy clothes left, much less something valuable. "I don't have anything," I muttered, feeling like everything was spiraling out of control.

"That's too bad." The prince tsked. "You broke into my castle and stole one of my possessions." He nodded once and the warriors advanced, the tip of their spears an inch from our bodies. "You are criminals and you'll be treated as such."

"Please, Prince Lark," Farrah started. "I'm sure we can come to an agreement. Just give us a chance."

The prince stepped down from the dais and took a couple

of steps toward Farrah. "You think that just because I'm in love with you and have been asking for your hand in marriage for years now that you can come in here, make a fool of me, and not pay for it?"

I gasped. Wyatt's face paled.

By the moon, what was he talking about?

"I know you don't have any use for that dagger," Farrah said. "It's just wasting away and gathering dust on your wall. Why not let us have it?"

The prince shook his head. "General Auron, take them to the dungeon."

The general raised his hand and the tips of the warriors' blades pressed against us.

"Wait!" Farrah lifted her chin, defiant. Determined. "I have something valuable to offer you in exchange for the dagger."

The prince's brows arched up. "And what is that?"

"Myself," Farrah said.

"What?" Wyatt barked.

"No, Farrah!" I yelled. From her body reactions, I knew how much she hated him. How could she give herself to him like that?

"You give us the dagger and let us walk out of here free and unharmed," Farrah said, "and I'll come back and marry you in three years' time."

One corner of the prince's lips curved up. "Three years. Hm, three years. That is a hiccup on our long lifetimes." He smiled at her, a wicked grin that chilled my bones. "Deal."

He extended his hand to her.

Wyatt slapped it away. "Farrah, no. Don't do it."

"I agree. This is nuts," I said.

"This is the only way." Farrah reached forward and slipped her hand into the prince's waiting one.

A swirl of ice and shadows surrounded us for three seconds, making me shiver in fear. As fast as it came, it was gone.

"It's done," the prince announced, retreating a few steps. The smug look on his face was nauseating. "General Auron, please hand the dagger to Lady Farrah."

Without ceremony, the general deposited the dagger in Farrah's hand.

"Thank you," Farrah whispered, hugging the dagger tight.

"A deal is a deal," the prince said, his tone colder than before. "If you aren't back in three years, you'll suffer the consequences."

A knot appeared between Farrah's brows. "I know very well how it works."

The prince waved his hand at us as if we were bugs infecting his fortress. "You may go now."

The warriors moved, forming a semicircle with the prince behind them. The general took the lead and escorted us out of the main hall, the warriors and their spears following us close.

In no time, we had been thrown out of the castle—with a magical dagger and a marriage deal.

As if it wanted to match our mood, the moon stayed behind thick cloud all night, and we trudged through the forest in the darkness. Wyatt and I could see well in the dark, but I wasn't so sure about fae. However, Farrah hadn't uttered a word since we left the fortress, and for some reason, every time she was quiet, I felt like respecting that.

Wyatt had other thoughts, though.

He halted and crowded over Farrah. "How could you do that?"

She bumped into him and staggered back. Wyatt grabbed her elbows. She shrugged, breaking his hold. "He's a powerful fae prince. He would have taken me eventually, one way or another. This way, I at least got something from him."

My gut twisted. "I don't get it. The dagger was for me. Why would you buy it with your life?"

"I thought we were friends," she said simply.

"Of course we are friends, but I would never ever put you in such a situation. You should have told us what we were getting into."

"Why didn't you tell us you knew him?" Wyatt asked, hurt lacing his words. "Why didn't you tell us he wanted to marry you?"

"That wouldn't have changed anything," Farrah insisted. Like me, Wyatt must have known how afraid and nervous she had been facing Lark. She had promised herself to a man she hated. A man she feared. "We went in, did what we had to do, and now we've got the dagger." She pushed it into my arms. "This belongs to you."

I stared at the dagger. "I feel like I should say thank you, but I'm really upset about how things turned out."

"You're welcome." Farrah sidestepped Wyatt. "Now, let's go back to Unity. We still have a full day of travel, and I really could use some sleep."

Farrah walked on. After letting out a grunt, Wyatt followed her.

I didn't move, entranced by the dagger of all hunting.

According to what I had been told, this dagger could be used to mark someone for death. If I used it to mark Isalia for death, it meant she would have to die. If she didn't, then the dagger would kill me instead.

That didn't sound like the best deal, but I didn't think I could live in a world where Isalia was a powerful alpha, who destroyed everything in her path, who killed my parents, and now threatened to take Unity.

I knelt on the ground. I held the dagger's hilt tight in my right hand and placed the tip of the blade on my left palm. I dragged the blade across my skin, making an X shape and thinking of the name of the supernatural I was marking for death.

Isalia.

The dagger didn't cut me. The lines forming the X shone white for a moment, then disappeared. Nothing was left behind, but I could feel it inside me. The X was inside me, counting away the days.

How long I had until it claimed my life instead, nobody knew. There wasn't a hard and fast rule. It could be weeks or a year. One thing was certain: the faster I killed her, the safer I would be.

"Luana?" Wyatt called. He and Farrah were already a ways ahead of me. "Where are you?"

"I'm coming!" I rose to my feet and slipped the dagger through my belt before taking off after my friends.

18

KEERAN

After having dinner and making up with my mother, I headed to my cabin. I had no idea when Luana would come back, but I couldn't help it. I sat down on the porch behind the cabin and looked up at the dark sky. I had developed a fondness for the moon, mostly because of Luana, and I hated not seeing it tonight. Its darkness made me think Luana was alone and lost in the forest, needing my help.

But she didn't come that night. Nor did she arrive the next day. I was going out of my mind with worry, but my mother kept assuring me the place Luana and the others had gone was far from here—well over a day from here. To go there and come back would take at least three days.

To pass the freaking time, I trained with my mother. When she was busy with the town, I either trained by myself, helped her, or checked on my father. He was still the same—an empty shell lying in the infirmary bed, staring at the ceiling, unmoving. If it weren't for the slow up and down of his chest, I would believe he was dead.

It saddened me to see him like that.

But the sadness was replaced by disgust. The fragments of his memories kept assaulting me—the witches he tortured, the warlocks he abused, the innocents he killed. It was a miracle I didn't curl into a ball in a corner and go mad. As mad as he had been.

At night, when my mother slept, all I could do was sit on the back porch and wait. The past two nights, I ended up falling asleep there, on the porch steps—there was a reason why my back had been hurting so much.

Finally, in the middle of the third night, I heard Luana arrive. I had thought she would have come from the backyard, as she usually did, but this time, she had come in the cabin through the front door.

I shot up and raced inside.

She was frozen a few feet from the door, watching me. She had probably heard me way before I had heard her.

"You're back and you're okay," I said, relieved. I was so freaking scared she would be hurt, I was going out of my mind.

She took a step back. "What are you doing here?"

I ran a hand through my hair. "Luana ..."

She retreated some more. "Don't Luana me. What the hell are you doing here?" Her voice rose.

Shit. I knew I had hurt her—I knew she hated me—but seeing it all without the haze of the amulet's magic broke my heart. I had done this to her. I had been a jerk. I had ripped her heart out.

Simple words wouldn't fix it, but it was all I had right now.

"I took off the amulet," I said, hoping my honesty would

break some of the wall she had rightfully erected between us. "Soren came out of it. I stole his magic. He's at the infirmary right now, being seen by the healer. He's a shell, and I hate seeing him like that, but it's done. The amulet is gone, and its darkness left me. I'm myself again."

A deep line marred her forehead. "As if that fixes all the crap you said to me."

"I know." I sighed. "I was a jerk and I hurt you, but you have to believe me, that wasn't me. Everything I said to you was a lie. It was the darkness talking. It wanted to hurt you, to push you away."

"It succeeded," she snapped.

"I know, and I accept whatever punishment you want to inflict on me, except pushing me out of your life." I felt like I was losing it. If I didn't say the right thing, if I didn't let her know how I felt, I would lose her once and for all. "I'm so sorry the darkness fed you lies, and you believed them, but I swear, they really were lies." Tears burned behind my eyes. "I can't live without you, Luana."

"Stop!" She lifted her index finger. "Just ... stop."

"Please, just listen to me." Holding my breath, I took a step closer to her. She didn't move. "You're my mate, Luana. Please listen to me."

She groaned. "I shouldn't have told you that."

"I'm glad you did, and honestly? I think I would have figured it out on my own if you hadn't told me. Because we're good together, Luana, you know that. You are my second half. My heart and soul. My soul mate."

"Please, Keeran, don't." She shook her head. "You hurt me. You really hurt me."

I should have prepared better. I should have written a

letter to her, lit thousands of candles around the cabin, spread rose petals on the floor, made her a nice romantic dinner, and prepared her a warm bubble bath. Anything. All those things. More. She deserved so much more than this stupid warlock.

"It wasn't me." I took another step toward her. "It really wasn't me. In my right mind, I would never say those things to you." I reached for her and wrapped her hands in mine. "I love you, Luana." She pulled back, but I held on tight. "I love you more than anything in this world." I tugged her to me. "Please, forgive me. Give me another chance." She resisted. "If you want, I'll get down on my knees and beg." I started kneeling, totally serious. For her, I would kiss the floor she walked on, even lick it.

But she stopped me. She held onto my hands and pulled me up. "That's ... enough," she whispered. "It's enough."

I stared at her. "Do you forgive me?"

She stared at me for a long time. "Say it one more time."

"What? I'll say anything for you, just tell me what."

"That you love me."

That was so freaking easy. I wrapped my arms around her, and fixed my eyes on hers. "I love you, Luana, more than life itself."

Slowly, I leaned into her. To my relief, she didn't pull back. She even gasped when I touched my lips to hers, brushing them lightly. I couldn't do slow and soft with Luana, though. Only she could bring out such lust and hunger from me—for her.

I covered her mouth with mine, and kissed her with all I had. She melted in my arms, her body pressing against mine.

Desire shot down low. A groan started in my chest as I broke the kiss and picked her up in my arms.

I watched her, my eyes glued to hers, as I carried her to the bedroom. Still staring at her, I deposited her on the bed. I didn't advance; I didn't pull back. I was too afraid of moving and being rejected.

The only thing I did was snap my fingers and light a side lamp, so I could see the goddess in my bed better.

My chest constricted with the intense gleam in Luana's eyes.

Then, to my relief, she grabbed the collar of my shirt, and pulled me to her. My body covered hers, but I still didn't dare kiss her again.

"I love you too," she whispered. She reached for the hem of my shirt and tugged it up. "Make love to me." Her voice was sultry, needy.

I groaned. Holy freaking mother ...

I took off my shirt and my pants, and worked on taking off her clothes too. Luana had a satisfied grin when I lay over her again—skin to skin, the way I liked.

She hooked her arms around my neck, and her legs around my waist, aligning her hips just right with my hard-on. I lowered my head to her throat, lost in the heat of desire and yearning agony and love.

Slowly, I slipped inside her, drawing a breathy gasp from her. The noises she made ... my blood heated more.

"This," I whispered, against her ear. I started moving again, slowly, agonizing, but delicious all the same. "This is paradise."

"I know." She reached down and clasped her hands on my ass, tugging me harder against her. I groaned again. "I do know."

I was lost in desire, but I had never been more complete.

No matter what happened, no matter where we went, no

matter what adversaries we faced, Luana would always be my safe harbor.

My home.

19

THE NEXT MORNING, I DIDN'T WANT TO GET OUT OF BED. IT seemed surreal that everything was going well. We had found the second item, and Keeran had gotten rid of the amulet. We had made up and made love all night long.

The only downside was that now Farrah was promised to a fae prince who could probably match Soren in his wickedness. I had asked her more about him during our trip back, but all she said was that he had been locked here on Earth, the same way she and her brother and their people had, and that he was not a good man.

I didn't feel great about this union. The one thing that kept me sane about it, though, was the fact that we had another three years to find a way to undo this deal.

Right now, we had other problems to deal with.

I finally got out of bed and went with Keeran for breakfast at Almae's house. As expected, Wyatt and Farrah were already there, but they both seemed in a worse mood. Both teenagers were seated at the table ends, as far away as they could be from each other, their arms crossed, their mouths pouting.

In the kitchen, Almae handed me two jars—one with ice tea, the other with orange juice. "Put these on the table, please." She leaned in closer. "And talk about something, anything, before those two freeze the entire house."

I almost laughed at her joke. However, Farrah was probably controlling her temper so that she really didn't freeze the house.

I took a place at the table and started passing out fruit, toast, and drinks, while trying to come up with a subject to talk about.

Farrah was faster, though. "We've got two items now. Any idea where the third could be?"

I suppressed a flinch. It wasn't like I didn't want to discuss our game plan, but the last three days had been eventful. We had scored a win, but also a loss. I had been avoiding talking about the dagger since it had been the cataclysm for the mood around the table.

"As long as it's not with another fae prince," Wyatt mumbled.

I shook my head. "I don't. I guess we need to research again."

Almae sat down on the table and placed a plateful of fresh pancakes in the center. "The crown of all branches. All I can think of is that it's hidden in a forest. Maybe a special forest."

"Actually," Keeran started. Seated by my side, he casually grabbed two pancakes and put them in his plate. "I think I know where it is."

We all stared at him.

"What do you mean?" I asked as curiosity ate my insides.

"When I absorbed my father's powers, I also took some of his memories." He shuddered. By the moon, I could only imagine how terrible most of those memories were. "He stumbled on the crown before, but he didn't think much of it."

My heartbeat sped up. "Where is it?"

"At the ruins of the old palace, where you used to live," he said. "Soren went there once. He saw the crown tangled among vines and broken furniture, but he thought it was part of the vegetation. He did sense power around it, but he couldn't pinpoint it to the crown, so he left it there."

My breath hitched. "You're telling me the crown has been wasting away at the old palace all this time? Nobody found it?"

He shrugged. "That was years ago. Someone might have found it after that, but I think we should go check it out."

I shot to my feet. "I'm ready."

Keeran grabbed my wrist and tugged me down. "The crown has been there for years. A few minutes to finish your breakfast and get properly dressed won't make a much difference."

I crossed my arms, feeling my temper rising. "Easy for you to say."

"He's right," Almae said, her voice soothing. "Eat something at least. Who knows what challenges you'll find retrieving this item. You'll need your strength."

"Fine," I snapped. I knew I was acting like a thirteen-year-old, but I couldn't help it. We knew where the crown was! I wanted to go after it now.

Keeran winked at me.

I wanted to punch him. I hated this new Keeran.

Not really. I was just upset that he was the level-headed one right now.

"Great." Almae smiled. "We can all enjoy a fine breakfast together before setting off. Again."

KEERAN WAS OUR GUIDE FOR THE TRIP. HE USED SOREN'S broken memories to take us to my first home, a place I didn't remember. It was supposedly close to the Dark Vale pack, but hidden and secured.

Since it took us over a day to go to Dark Vale, we hiked out of the mountains, borrowed a car, and went as far as we could with it. Once we had no other choice but go back into the forest on foot, we abandoned the car on the side of the road, hoping it would be found and returned to its owner, and moved on.

Here, clouds traveled through the sky, covering the moon often. Since we started hiking up through the forest, Keeran spelled sticks with cool flames at their tip, and we used them as torches. Wyatt and I might not need the light to see in the dark, but Keeran and Farrah did.

It was past four in the morning when we finally arrived in Dark Vale territory.

I halted at a path I knew well and turned to Keeran. "Where to now?"

He gestured to our left, off the path. "A few more miles this way."

I cursed under my breath.

A few more miles? It would be morning when we arrived, and we wouldn't have slept for over twenty-four hours—and that was after a three-day hike to retrieve the dagger. If we encountered enemies or booby traps, we would be too tired to fight.

We marched on.

I tried keeping my anticipation, excitement, and nervousness to myself. I was going to see the place I was born, where my parents wanted to raise me, the place I was supposed to rule. What would it look like? What would I feel? On top of that, I was heading toward the last item on the list. If I found the crown and joined it with the three other items, I would have my powers back.

It sounded unbelievable even to my ears.

Almost two hours later, when the sun's faint orange rays started peeking on the horizon, Keeran slowed down. He pushed aside some low tree branches and said, "I present you, the Starlight Vale."

I stepped past the branches and stared at the endless valley ... and the destruction spread across it. At first, it took me a moment to place it all, but there were buildings in the valley, and most of them had caved-in roofs and vegetation crawling up the sides, as if the vines and trees couldn't tell the stone that made up the buildings and the forest apart.

The sun rose a little higher, the rays blinding me for a second.

An image flashed in my mind.

A beautiful town made of gray stone and dark wood. Trees that grew alongside buildings, weaving the branches around the corners and up the walls, becoming part of the structures. Green leaves, purple and midnight blue flowers planted along the streets in neatly cut flowerbeds.

And in the center of it all, the tall and proud palace. Like the rest of the town, it was made of stone and trees, but it extended up, toward the sky, as if it could reach the stars and the moon.

I blinked.

The towers were gone. No building was taller than the others among the rubble now.

My heart sank a little.

Farrah stopped by my side. "Are you okay?"

I nodded, not sure I could explain what had happened. Had it been a memory? Or was it magic, making me see what the town once was?

I didn't know.

"This way." Keeran beckoned us to follow him down a path covered in soot and dirt. If he didn't know of it because of Soren's memories, we would have never found it.

He led us down the path until we were at the edge of town—at the edge of the destruction.

"What happened here?" Wyatt asked.

"I don't know," I whispered. Just as I said the words, another image flashed in my mind.

The ground shook hard. The walls cracked; the branches snapped. People ran, screaming and gathering their loves ones. Fleeing.

"Are you sure you're okay?" Farrah asked, bringing me back to the present. "You're a little pale."

"Seeing her home in this state must be hard," Keeran offered. Since his statement was true, I nodded again, but didn't say anything. "Last time Soren saw the crown, it was in the palace."

"The palace is in the middle of all the rubble," I said. "In the center of the town."

Keeran narrowed his eyes at me. "You remembered?"

I stared at the narrow street in front of us. With all the

crumbled houses, fallen trees, and outgrown vegetation, it wouldn't be easy to reach the palace. "I don't think it can be called that."

"What do you mean?" Wyatt asked.

"Let's just go," I said, walking forward. I wanted to get the crown and go. Being in here, seeing these images, it was messing with my mind.

Keeran grabbed my arm. "We have to be careful. One wrong step, and the remains of these buildings might fall on us."

I gently unwrapped his fingers from around my arm. "I'll be careful."

If he was upset about my sudden coldness, he didn't show it. I was glad he wasn't pushing, because honestly, not even I was sure of what was going on with me right now. There were too many emotions swirling inside me, and I couldn't make sense of them all, much less all of them together.

So, I shoved them all down and marched ahead.

Keeran, Wyatt, and Farrah followed closely. A couple of times, pebbles rolled, the walls crumbled, the branches bent. I was sure we wouldn't leave this place without an injury or two.

My gut tightened as I realized the hardest part probably lay ahead. If there were booby traps around the crown, they could have been deployed a long time ago. Or not properly aligned.

I imagined a hundred arrows shooting through a narrow corridor, with only one safe passage. If the earthquake had moved either the walls or the arrows, then maybe there was no safe passage now.

We walked down what was supposed to be one of the main streets leading to the palace. The pavement was broken, the trees had fallen across it, and in some places, the sides of the buildings had come down, littering the way.

As we neared the palace, I braced myself. I stepped over the fallen wooden gates, the overgrown grass, the broken steps, past the missing doors, and into the foyer.

Another flash filled my mind.

Little me with unruly brown hair, running across the foyer, my bare feet slipping on the smooth gray floors, and my father running after me. My giggles echoed through the place, my father's deep laughter following. He caught me with a swoop of his big arm and propped me up on his shoulders.

A gasp tore through my throat as I took a good look at his face. Most of his features were rough and manly, but I had his soft eyes and his big smile. His long hair looked like mine too.

Tears brimmed in my eyes.

"Luana?"

I blinked and saw the foyer with cracked floors, fallen wooden chandelier, dust, and lots of vines.

"What happened?" Keeran asked. "It was like ... you weren't here."

"I've been seeing images," I confessed as a tear rolled down my face. "Ever since we arrived outside the valley, I've been seeing images of how the town used to be. Of what the palace looked like." I took a deep breath, trying to calm myself. "Of my father and I."

"Like memories?" Farrah asked.

"I think so? I don't know." I shrugged. "Perhaps it's not my memories, but the place's memory." That sounded absurd. "I don't know." I wiped my tears away and glanced at Keeran. "Where to now?"

"The main hall." He pointed to the broken archway across the foyer.

The archway opened to a long and wide corridor. At the end of the corridor, another archway awaited. Keeran, Farrah, and Wyatt entered the main hall, but I paused at the entrance.

I knew another nugget of memory would greet me here.

I was ready this time.

The main hall was like a throne room, but for the Starlight werewolves, it was a little different. The alpha's chair was the biggest one with thick wood and dark blue velvet seats. Two smaller chairs flanked it, for the alpha's family. Directly across from those three chairs, several smaller chairs spread out in a semicircle.

My father was seated in his chair, his thick brows knotted.

My mother paced in front of him, with little me in her arms, my head on her shoulder, sleeping.

Despite the nervous look she had on her face, I couldn't help starting at my beautiful mother. Her features were delicate, her brown eyes warm, and her cheekbones high. She had her hair tied in a loose braid, purple flowers weaved through the knots. She wore leather pants and a beautiful dark blue blouse.

"Calm down, my love," my father said.

"I can't calm down," my mother replied. "I know something will happen. Something bad. I can feel it."

"I never doubt your intuition." My father rose and stepped in front of my mother, forcing her to stop pacing. "If something bad happens, we'll be ready for it. I'll make sure of it."

There was a desperate glint in her eyes. "How? I don't even know what will happen."

"I will look everywhere," my father said, still calm. "I'll find whatever it is, before it finds us." He placed his hands on her shoulders. "Now, please, calm down. You'll wake up our little wolf." He leaned down and placed a soft kiss on my forehead.

"I'm worried about her," my mother whispered.

My father stared into her eyes. "I'll never let anything bad happen to her."

A sob echoed in my ears.

The image was gone.

Keeran, Wyatt, and Farrah were standing a few feet from me, looking at me as if I had sprouted wings and horns—impossible traits for a werewolf.

"Another memory?" Wyatt asked.

"Yes," I rasped, realizing the sob I had heard had been mine. My eyes were full of unshed tears. "I saw my father, my mother, and me." I pointed to the center of the room, where the chairs still were located, but under piles of broken ceiling, fallen wooden chandeliers, dust, and vines. "Right there."

Keeran walked up to me and put an arm around my shoulders. "Do you want to talk about it?"

I shook my head. "I would rather get the damn crown and leave." That wasn't true. I kind of wanted to keep seeing my parents and me and our brief life together, but I wasn't sure how much more of it my heart could take. "Where did you see it?"

"Here." He gestured to the center of the room, where I had pointed to.

I walked closer without stepping over anything and looked around. "I don't see anything."

"Exactly."

I frowned at him. "What do you mean?"

He walked over the rubble until he was right beside one of the fallen chandeliers. It was broken in several pieces, and even then, the thing was almost as big as Keeran. Branches twisted around, forming a big spiral. Smaller branches sprouted from the main one, twisted around candle-like lights, most of them lost or broken now. With a sly grin, Keeran reached for the top part of the spiral, where it became a smaller circle of twisted branches.

But the moment he touched it, a zap echoed through the room and he went flying back.

"Keeran!" I screamed, rushing to him.

He groaned as he sat up. He had landed on a fallen painting, near the wall. "Shit, that hurt."

"Are you okay?" I hovered over him, looking for any wounds.

A hand on the wall, Keeran stood. "It hurt like a bitch, but I'll live."

"What happened?" Wyatt asked from behind me.

Keeran rolled his shoulders, as if shaking off the shock that had sent him flying. "That's the crown. I think it's protected." He looked at me. "I guess only someone who is destined to have it can grab it."

I gulped. That was the crown? A bunch of coiled branches? On top of a chandelier? And I had to get it? And risk getting shocked too?

What was I saying? I wasn't afraid. Getting shocked and thrown across the room was a small price to pay for retrieving the crown and becoming the alpha of the Starlight pack.

With determined steps, I walked over the rubble and stood beside the broken chandelier. My fingers trembled as I reached for the top. Bracing myself, I touched the branches with two fingers. Nothing happened. I closed my hand around the circle of branches and pulled. It cracked, as if I had taken a piece of the chandelier apart. I stared at the thing in my hand.

This was the crown? Really? It looked like a circle of branches a child would have woven together, not a powerful crown. I looked at Keeran. "Are you sure this is it?"

He nodded. "I think so. When Soren came here, he felt power coming from it, but it was faint. He believed it was the magic from the lights that had been stored in the chandeliers. But when I was looking closer at his memories, I realized that, out of the five chandeliers in this room, this is the only one with that top part. It was also the only one that still had magic in it." He jerked his chin to the circle in my hand. "I can still feel some magic in it."

"Some magic?" I glanced at the crown again. I bet I could snap it in two if I applied a little pressure. "You mean little magic? This is supposed to be a powerful item."

"I know, and to be honest, that's the only part I'm not so sure about," he admitted.

"Put it on," Farrah said. "If it is the crown of all branches, I bet you'll feel something when you put it on."

Wyatt shrugged. "It's worth a try."

I glanced at Farrah and Wyatt. Despite everything going on between them, it was nice to see them agreeing on something, even if it was about this.

I returned my attention to the crown. It seemed so fragile and rotten and spiky. Holding my breath, I raised it high and placed it on my head.

A whirlwind of power enveloped me, ruffling my hair and my clothes. I stilled as the crown moved, as if fitting around my head.

By the moon, this really was the crown of all branches.

Keeran stared at me with proud eyes. "You unlocked it. Now I can feel it. The power in the crown is immense."

"It's beautiful," Farrah said, with a little smile.

Beautiful? She was crazy. I took the crown off. Upon touching it, I felt it was different, but I was surprised seeing it had changed. The wooden crown had transformed into a beautiful and slim dark blue metal circlet.

In my hands, the crown trembled and became a bunch of woven branches again. "What the ...?"

"It's amazing," Farrah whispered.

"What now?" Wyatt asked. "That's the third item. Do you feel your magic back?"

I frowned, disappointed. "No."

"Since you needed the three objects, maybe you need them all together," Keeran said. "We should go back to Unity and gather them all."

The disappointment was replaced by hope again. That seemed like a good idea. "Let's go."

20

KEERAN

IT WAS THE MIDDLE OF THE NIGHT WHEN WE ARRIVED BACK IN Unity. We hadn't slept in two freaking nights—and after a short break, another three if we counted the days Luana, Wyatt, and Farrah had been gone when they went to retrieve the dagger. I had stayed behind, but I hadn't slept much either. In the end, we were exhausted. The only thing that kept us going was the anticipation of putting the three objects together and finding out what happened.

The four of us went directly to the cabin Luana and I shared. Luana left the crown of all branches on the coffee table, then rushed to the bedroom, where she got the mirror of all seeing and the dagger of all hunting.

I could see how tense and nervous she was as she deposited the objects side by side on the coffee table. She stepped back and stared at them.

Nothing happened.

"What's going on?" she asked, irritation lacing her words. "These are the three damn items. Where's my magic?"

"Maybe you have to put on the crown on and hold the

others." Farrah shrugged. "You know, like you activated the crown when it was in your head."

I nodded. "I bet that's it."

Sucking a sharp breath, Luana put on the crown. Instantly, it transformed into the dark blue diadem. Then, she held the dagger in one hand and the mirror in another.

Instantly, the objects shone a dark purple light and magic filled the room. Luana started shifting, but instead of turning into her usual black wolf, she turned into a beautiful dark blue one, with a soft coat and bright white eyes. The objects fell on the floor, but the magic remained.

It was done.

Luana was now a real Starlight wolf.

"You did it," I said, proud of her.

She jumped over the couch, then spun around a couple of times, like a child with a new toy. I couldn't help but smile.

Wyatt turned off the lights, and I gasped. Luana shone a dark blue light, as if her skin was neon. It illuminated the entire room, as if she were a bright star.

It was stunning.

She was freaking stunning.

Wyatt turned the light back on, and Luana shifted back into her human form, her clothes intact, and a huge grin on her beautiful face. "I did it!" Just then, a blue crescent moon flashed on her forehead. Luana gasped. "I really did it!"

"Now you can claim the Starlight pack," Farrah said, her tone excited. She, too, was happy for Luana.

Wyatt, though, was quiet. A deep line marred his forehead. What could be the problem? Was he still upset about what he had done in the past under Soren's orders? Was it because of Farrah's promise to the fae prince? Or was it something else?

Before I could ask him, Luana grabbed the three items in her arms and headed to the door. "I'm going to the Starlight den right now." I was in desperate need of a shower and sleep. She glanced over her shoulder and batted her lashes at me. "Are you guys coming?"

How the hell was I supposed to say no to her? "Sure."

Wyatt cleared his throat. "Actually, if you don't mind, I'm going to stay." He glanced at her, but he didn't hold his gaze. "You don't need me for this next part, and I'm really tired."

"Oh." Luana's brows curled down. "It's okay. Sure, I don't mind."

Farrah frowned too. "Um, I'm going to stay too."

If I knew anything about Farrah, she was staying behind to keep an eye on Wyatt. Which was great, because with the way he had been depressed and quiet lately, Luana and I were worried about him. It was good if someone kept him company, even if he didn't want it.

"Sure," I said. "You two should rest. We'll let you know if anything happens in the morning."

I pushed Luana out of the cabin. She made a face at me, but didn't say anything. When we were at the edge of the forest in the backyard, she finally whispered, "What was that?"

"I think Wyatt is still upset about Farrah's promise," I said, equally low. With a werewolf hearing, we had to be careful so that Wyatt couldn't hear us, even from here.

"Oh, he'll be upset about that for a long time." She let out a sigh. "It sucks, you know? First, the terrible things he did for Soren. And now, Farrah, the only person I thought could actually help him, goes and stabs him in the back. He must be devastated." She glanced at the objects in her arms. "You know what? Perhaps we should stay with them, and do this tomorrow morning."

I shook my head. "There's only three hours until tomorrow morning. Besides, they might be teenagers, but I don't think they will do anything stupid. We should leave them alone to figure things out by themselves. We'll step in if necessary."

Luana stared at me for a moment, clearly torn about the topic. "Fine," she muttered. "Let's go claim my pack."

With a smile, she took off, running into the forest.

I chuckled and ran after her.

I HADN'T BEEN IN THE STARLIGHT DEN BEFORE, AND I HADN'T seen any other Starlight wolf before other than Luana a few minutes ago. Seeing them all at the bottom of this huge cave, glowing like neon sticks, was surreal.

A couple shifted into their human forms and approached us.

"Romulus is the current leader of the pack," Luana explained. "And Meira is his mate."

The tall black man halted right in front of me, and glanced up and down, sizing me up.

"You're Luana's mate," he said. Not a question.

"I am." I stood tall, wanting to show him I could hold my own. "My name is Keeran."

"But you're a warlock," Meira said, her gray eyes suspicious.

"Yeah, well, it happened that way," Luana said.

"You want to be alpha of our pack with a warlock for a mate?" Romulus asked.

I could see as Luana's temper rose. Her face hardened and her shoulders squared. She took a step forward, defying them. "I am the damn alpha of the Starlight pack, and who is or isn't my mate isn't your concern." She dipped her chin to the three objects she was holding. "Now, here are your three items." She shoved the objects in Romulus arms. "And this."

Luana shifted into a Starlight wolf. Gasps and low barks resonated within the cave. Magic flashed. The werewolves lowered their heads. Romulus and Meira folded onto one knee.

"My alpha," Romulus whispered.

"Welcome home," Meira said.

Luana shifted back—her clothes intact. That was some neat magic.

The dark blue crescent shone in her forehead again. Romulus and Meira ran their finger down their foreheads, in a crescent shape, leaving behind a trail of blue light. The crescent moon gleamed on the wolves' forehead throughout the den. Then, it was gone.

Luana looked around the room. "My wolves, I don't want us to hide anymore. I want us to rise and take back our home. I want us to rebuild the Starlight Vale and start anew." Low howls filled the cavern. I hoped they were signs of agreement. "But before we can do that, the she-wolf who killed my parents and destroyed our pack is threatening all supernaturals. We need to defeat her." She paused. "Will you fight with me?"

This time, the howls were loud and long.

Romulus answered, "We'll go to war with you, my alpha."

WE REMAINED AT THE STARLIGHT DEN FOR A WHILE. LUANA and I got together with Romulus, Meira, and other higher ranked wolves. We explained to them the entire situation: Isalia was pregnant, and until she had the baby, we had to wait to attack. Meanwhile, Romulus and Meira would train with Luana, teach her how to channel and use her unique magic, so she would be ready and strong when she faced Isalia.

When we got back to our cabin, the sun was already up, and I could barely feel my legs.

I planned on pushing Luana down in bed, snuggling with her, and sleeping all day.

However, my mother had other plans. She was waiting for us at our cabin. "Now that you're well, it's time for you to become a leader too," she said.

I narrowed my eyes. "What do you mean?"

"There are a handful of warlocks in Unity," she said. "As the warlock lord, you should talk to them. You could even order them to join you, but—"

"I won't do that," I said, shaking my head. "I won't force anyone to do what they don't want to. I don't want to be that kind of leader."

A small smile spread over her lips. "That's exactly what I wanted to hear. Now go talk to them."

"What? Now? We haven't slept in over two days." Not to mention the other three nights I barely slept while I anxiously waited for Luana.

"I know," she said, as if staying awake for over forty-eight hours was no big deal. "But you'll sleep much better once you talked to them and convinced them to join your side." She glanced at Luana. "Right? Won't you rest better now that you have found your pack, and you know they will have your back?"

"Yes," Luana said, dragging out the S. I knew she didn't want to disagree with my mother, but she was also too tired to take another step.

"See? I'm right." My mother waved at us. "Now go talk to them."

I groaned. "Seriously, we still have a month until Isalia gives birth. This can wait until tomorrow."

She shook her head. "Keeran, just do it."

I wanted to stomp around and yell at her and rage that I wouldn't do it. But I knew she would keep bugging me, and not letting me sleep, until I did it. Why had I been so eager to find my mother when she nagged me nonstop? Never mind. Despite everything, I was glad I had found her.

And because of that, I dragged my feet down the hill, to the school building near the marketplace. My mother had already called the warlocks for a meeting, and they were waiting for me.

With Luana by my side, I walked into the classroom and found eight warlocks seated at the desks, like students waiting for a teacher. I had seen most of them around town before. The warlocks ranged in age from early twenties to fifties, but they all seemed capable and strong. I could feel their magic in the air.

I bet they could feel mine too.

"The warlock lord," Finch said. He was the oldest, with gray hair and a few wrinkles around his dark eyes. He was a potion master, and his teas were sought by every supernatural in town. "You finally defeated your father."

I halted in front of the desks, doing my best to look composed and alert. "Something like that."

"Almae said you wanted to talk to us," Boise said. He was younger, probably the youngest of all of us. He had shaggy, sand blond hair and green eyes. "What about?"

I would start this in a different way. "Why are you in Unity?"

The warlocks exchanged glances. "What do you mean?"

"Soren was a strong warlock lord, and the warlocks seemed to worship him," I said. "Why didn't you stick with him? Why did you come to Unity?"

"Soren was crazy, okay?" Aspen snapped. He had long dark dreadlocks, and tattoos covering his arms and neck. "He was batshit. He murdered supernaturals right and left."

"And the witches," Ray said. He had short black hair and a messy beard. "He hunted witches like they were animals. Then, he locked them up and abused them." He shuddered.

"He was evil," Finch said.

I nodded. "Soren is gone now, but a she-wolf, as evil and mad as he was, took his place. She commands an army comprised of hungry werewolves and powerful warlocks, and she wants us dead." I gestured to Luana and me. "We'll fight her. We'll win. We'll claim our warlocks and our werewolves back. We'll teach them good from evil, and we'll punish the ones who don't want to learn. We'll restore peace and glory to all of our races."

"That's good, I guess," Boise said.

"What does that have to do with us?" Ray asked.

"If we don't go after her and stop her, Isalia will come for Unity," Luana said. "She'll destroy everything and everyone. She'll kill our families and friends."

The warlocks muttered their discontentment.

"We can stop her," I said, shushing them. "But I need your help. I need you to join us and fight with us."

The mutters started again.

"I'm sorry, but I'm out," Finch said. He rose from his seat. "I'm too old for this. I would rather live my life and brew my teas without getting involved in any fights."

"There won't be any life to live if we don't stop Isalia," Luana said. "She'll destroy Unity. She'll destroy us. She'll destroy you."

The old man glared at Luana, but didn't say anything. Without a word, he marched out of the classroom.

"Tell me," Boise said. "What can seven warlocks do against Isalia and her army?"

"We already have an army of our own," I said. "But the more, the merrier. Warlocks are powerful and unique. If you join us, our chances of winning will only increase."

They glanced at each other again.

"Don't you want to protect your family? Your friends? Your home?" Luana asked. "The only way to do that is to fight with us."

Aspen sighed. "What the hell, I'm in."

Boise nodded. "Me too."

The other five agreed.

Pride and satisfaction bloomed inside me. It seemed I, too, had an army.

21

MAPS AND NOTES AND OTHER THINGS COVERED THE DINING table at the cabin. For the last month, Keeran and I analyzed them several times per day, testing several plans and strategies. Choosing one. Refining it. Testing it. Modifying it.

A month had passed since I had reclaimed my pack, and the warlocks of Unity had join us. I had spent the time training with Romulus and Meira, and Keeran had been practicing with his warlocks—they hadn't really used magic and fought in years. Some of them came to Unity as children or teenagers and had never fought at all.

A Starlight wolf's magic was much different from a witch's or a warlock's. My magic made me stronger and faster than a normal werewolf. The darker the night, the brighter the moon, the stronger I was.

That was why we were planning on attacking Isalia in a week's time, during the full moon's peak.

Yesterday, a messenger had arrived with news from Isalia. She had given birth to a son. Keeran had a half-brother. A half-werewolf, half-warlock. I still felt nauseated when I thought about killing the innocent baby's mother, but what other choice did I have? It was either that, or let him be raised by her, which would certainly make him evil too.

Besides, if I didn't stop her, she would destroy us all. I couldn't allow that.

I pointed to the map of the Chateau of the Cursed and surrounding areas. "We'll surround the chateau on all sides."

Keeran, Wyatt, and Farrah leaned over the map.

"My warlocks and I can take the east side," Keeran said.

"If you give me half the wolves, I can take the south side," Wyatt said.

"Make that one third," Farrah. "Then I'll take the west side with a third, and you take the north side with the other third."

"Sounds good." I nodded. "We'll block all exits, then I'll challenge Isalia. She'll have to accept. Once she comes out and we start fighting, you guys storm in. Try to disarm or stun everyone, but no killing. We want to start a new era."

"Sounds good enough," Farrah said.

"Perhaps you should plan for surprises," Almae said from the kitchen. She had come earlier to make lunch for us—lots of finger food that we could eat while planning. "There are always surprises."

"True," I said, reaching for a spinach puff from over the kitchen counter. "So, what surprises could we have?"

"Hm, they are called surprises for a reason," Wyatt said, as if I was crazy.

"I know." I fought the urge to roll my eyes at him. "Still, we can try to guess what Isalia will do."

"All right, what would I do if I were an evil she-wolf in a dark castle?" Farrah asked in a teasing tone. She shoved a cheese roll in her mouth.

I chuckled. "Farrah, I'm serious."

"I know, but you have to admit that was funny." She winked.

I rolled my eyes at her. "Maybe."

The clatter of glass shattering made me jump back, ready to shift and summon my magic. But I tensed for a totally difference reason, when I realized it had been Almae. She swayed toward the kitchen counter, the shards of a broken plate all spread around her feet.

"Mother!" Keeran rushed to her. Careful with the shards, he grabbed her shoulders and steered into living room. He pushed her down on the sofa and sat down beside her. "What happened? Are you okay?"

Wyatt and I hovered over them, while Farrah went to the kitchen.

Almae put a hand on her temple and groaned. "I've had a headache since I woke up this morning," she said, her voice faint. Her complexion was pale, and her arms shook slightly.

"Do you want me to call the healer?" I offered.

Almae shook her head. "No, there's nothing she can do for me."

"What do you mean?" Keeran asked, concern obvious in his tone.

Farrah came back from the kitchen with a glass full of water and offered it to Almae.

The witch grabbed the glass from the young fae. "Thank you, my dear," Almae said. She took a long sip of the water.

"Mother, tell us what's going on," Keeran insisted.

"Visions," Almae mumbled. "I've been having complex but blurry visions since I woke up. Because there have been many, and I can't figure out what they mean, a deep headache started. No medicine or magic will help me, until I can tell what the visions are showing me."

I sat down on the coffee table. "Is there any way we can help?"

"No," she said with a sigh. "All you can do for now is prepare, because despite not being able to decipher these prophecies, I can tell you this: It means something big, something bad is about to happen."

A cold chill ran down my spine.

I didn't like the sound of that.

Keeran's eyes met mine. He was worried about what that meant, but he was more worried about this mother.

"You should take your mother to rest," I suggested. "We can continue this tomorrow."

He nodded at me, relieved at my understanding. "Come on." He hooked his arm underneath Almae's and helped her up. "Let's get you home."

Gentle and caring, Keeran helped Almae out.

When they closed the door and I finally stripped my attention from them, I looked back and found Farrah sweeping the kitchen. "You didn't need to do that."

She shrugged. "I don't mind." She picked up the shards and threw them in the trash. "So, are we continuing our meeting without Keeran?"

I shook my head. "No, no reason why we should." I waved them off. "Go. Spend some quality time together. Have fun."

Wyatt and Farrah stared at each other. As far as I knew, they could even be sharing the same cabin, but they had barely spoken the past month. Wyatt seemed deeper in his depression, except for when we were talking strategies. However, we soon would embark on the fight of our lives, and I really wanted to see Wyatt and Farrah patch things up. I knew nothing had happened between them, not even a kiss, but I also knew they liked each other. Everyone knew. I just hoped they could get past whatever was in their way and make up before it was too late.

Wyatt's cheeks flushed. "I'll just ... go ..." He turned on his heels and walked out of the cabin through the back door.

Farrah let out a long sigh and followed him.

Alone, I found I had nothing to do either. I wouldn't train with Romulus and Meira until this evening, which meant I had a few hours to do whatever I wanted.

Well, one thing I hadn't done in a while was to go out on a mindless run. That would certainly relax my muscles and clear my head. I shifted—it was so cool to be able to shift without worrying about clothes!—and left the house.

I ran into the forest and let my paws take me wherever they wanted.

22

KEERAN

IN THE END, I CAVED AND CALLED THE HEALER. MY MOTHER didn't look well—pale, nervous, with sweat on her forehead and hands—and I couldn't sit by doing nothing. The healer came in and gave her some tea.

"It'll knock her out," the witch healer said. "She'll wake up tomorrow."

"But she'll be fine?" I asked

The healer nodded. "Let's just hope that when she wakes up, these visions are gone."

The healer left soon after, and I stayed beside my mother's bed, watching over her for a little while more. At first, I was afraid to leave her alone, but after a couple of hours, I realized she was in a deep sleep, and if the healer was right, she wouldn't wake up anytime soon. So, I went back to my cabin.

Luana was probably in the forest, training with Romulus and Meira. Wanting to see her, I packed a light diner for us and head out to the clearing where she usually trained.

When I arrived, they had already finished.

"You've improved a lot, my alpha," Romulus said, a hint of pride in his voice, bowing his head.

"I'm sure you'll be able to defeat the evil she-wolf," Meira said, smiling. She also bowed her head to her alpha.

It was amazing to watch them. The Starlight wolves weren't like the other werewolves. The alpha was like a king or queen, and the mantle passed by blood. The other wolves could sense the alpha. They had uttermost respect and admiration for their alpha. I confessed I had been a little worried about Luana, since she was female and younger than most of them, but so far, they had supported her and treated her like a queen.

"You don't know Isalia," Luana said. "She uses dirty tricks. It won't be easy."

"We'll be ready for her," I said.

Luana smiled at me. "I heard you coming a mile away."

I frowned at her. "I don't think the cabin is even a mile away from here."

Her smile widened at my joke.

Romulus and Meira bowed again and took their leave.

Smile fading, Luana walked toward me. "How's your mother?"

"Sleeping," I said. "I called the healer and she gave her something to sleep. Apparently, she won't be up until tomorrow morning."

A deep knot appeared between Luana's brows. "That's a good thing, right? I mean, she needs to rest. Maybe she'll wake up without a headache or crazy visions."

I nodded. "That's what the healer said."

Luana stared at me, then at the wicker basket in my hand. "What's that?"

"I brought dinner." I lifted the basket. "A picnic in the

moonlight." Although, it was getting awfully dark. I snapped my fingers together, and a small bonfire of deep red flames appeared. "And candlelight. Of sorts."

She smiled at me. "Keeran, I never thought you were this romantic."

I chuckled. "I didn't know it either. Until you."

Luana's cheek reddened.

How could I resist her when she was being so freaking cute and sexy at the same time? I reached for her, but before I could wrap my arms around her waist and pull her to me, Luana took the basket from me and stepped back. Clueless that I had been about to kiss her, Luana took the blanket out of the basket and spread it out on the grass in the center of the clearing, right beside the fake bonfire.

On this unusually warm night, under the starry sky, and enveloped by the scent of the trees and flowers, Luana sat down on the blanket and patted the spot right next to her. Like a puppy, I sat beside her.

"Let's see what we have here." She spied inside the basket.

There had been leftover chicken pot pie in the fridge. I had heated it up and put it in a sealed container, hoping the heat would maintain for a little while. I threw in some salad and toasted bread and softened spread, a bottle of wine and glasses, and hoped it was enough.

"You know I can't cook much," I said.

She took out the bottle of wine. "It looks good to me."

I smiled at her. How could I be so lucky? She was beautiful, kind, fun, caring, and I had almost lost her because of the darkness that had consumed me. Despair snaked around my chest at the thought. I didn't know how I could live without her. I didn't want to. I pushed those terrible thoughts out of my mind. She was here now with me. Nothing would happen.

I opened the wine bottle and poured the red liquid in the two glasses. Luana and I clinked our glasses and drank a long swallow.

She lowered her glass and stared at the flickering flames of the bonfire. "This is it," she said, her tone serious. "I've used the dagger of all hunting. I've marked Isalia for death."

My heart stopped. "You did what?" If I remembered correctly, if she marked someone for death and that person didn't die, then she would die instead. "Why would you do that?"

"Because I don't have a choice." She turned her hazel eyes to me. "Isalia has to die. I wish there was a way to immobilize her like you did with your father, but I don't believe I can take her werewolf genes out of her, or her evilness." She paused. "One of us will die soon."

I held her hand in mine. "That won't happen. I won't let you die."

Luana shook her head. "You know that's not how it works. I have to take her down by myself."

"But you're already the alpha of the Starlight pack. You don't need to become alpha of her pack too."

"I know, but if I don't become alpha of her pack, no one will be able to control her she-wolves. They will keep fighting until we're forced to kill them all, and I would rather stop with one death."

That made sense, but ... "There has to be another way."

"Besides that, I need to do this." She set the wine down and pressed her hand on her chest. "For me. She killed my parents; she tried to kill me as a child. Moreover, she broke my pride when she won that challenge from me."

"But she cheated."

"It doesn't matter. She still won. I'll only be able to have peace of mind if I win. The right way. No cheating." She gave me a pointed glance. I knew what she meant. Drake and I had once cheated, and helped her win against Uric, Isalia's mate. "That means, you can't help me. Even if I'm dying, you can't help me."

I shook my head. "Luana, you can't ask that of me."

"I'm not asking, Keeran. I'm telling you. You won't help me. Not this time."

How could she say that? Didn't she know how much I loved her? How much she mattered to me? I couldn't stand there and watch her die. "Luana—"

"One more thing," she said, interrupting me. "If I die, you have to promise you'll take care of everything. You'll take care of Unity, and you'll help my pack get back their home. They will have to move on and choose a new alpha, but I'm certain that if they are pointed in the right direction, they can do it."

"I don't like when you talk like that."

She reached to me and rested her hand on my cheek. "Hopefully, nothing like that will happen, but I would like to be prepared." I placed my hand on hers, holding hers in place, wishing I never had to let go. "Promise me. Promise me you won't help me, even if I die."

My throat went dry. "I can't promise that."

"Please, Keeran." The glint in her eyes, the pleading tone in her voice.

My next words practically broke my heart. "I promise."

Luana let out a long, relieved sigh. "Thank you."

She was thankful that I might have to let her die? No, that wasn't fair. She had to live. We all had to live. We were young, and because of our powers, we would live long lives. And I wanted to live with her.

My chest squeezed, and I was suddenly certain. Despite being sent by fate and being my mate, I was certain that she was the love of my life. I couldn't and wouldn't live without her.

I picked a grass blade from the ground and got up on one knee. "Luana, I love you more than everything in this entire world." Her eyes widened. "Please ... will you marry me?"

She gasped. "Keeran ..."

"All you have to say is yes or no."

Tears brimmed in her eyes and a smile spread over her lips. "Yes!"

My heart squeezed again, but this time in delight. I took her hand and placed it on my knee. Then, I tied the grass blade on her ring finger. I sent my magic into the grass blade, and it transformed into a black ring with a red stone in the center.

Luana stared at the ring. "It's beautiful." She scooted closer to me and wrapped her arms around me. "I love you."

Holding her tight, I leaned into her. "I love you more."

I pressed my lips to hers, kissing her slow, but deep. Luana moaned against my mouth, and I almost lost it right then. In a swift move, I laid her down on the blanket and claimed her. I claimed all of her.

***

IT WAS PAST MIDNIGHT WHEN LUANA AND I MADE OUR WAY BACK to our cabin. Holding my hand, Luana still teased me about being a sappy romantic. As far as I knew, werewolves didn't usually get engaged. Once they found their mates and accepted them, a celebration was held, sort of like a wedding ceremony, and that was it. Vampires were similar, though most didn't have true mates, and witches never got married, though they sometimes had partners—though Thea married Drake, but that was because they wanted to celebrate their love in a grand way. I would take a guess that warlocks also didn't marry, but that might be because most of them had been under the thumb of an evil leader so far.

I didn't know much about fae, though with Farrah's situation, I believed being engaged and having a big wedding party was the norm.

I wasn't sure what Luana would want to do—a small, intimate event, or a big ceremony. As long as she was beside me for the rest of my life, I didn't really care. However, now wasn't the time to discuss it. We had to worry about the fight ahead before we could plan our future.

I frowned.

"What's going on inside that handsome head?" she asked when we reached our backyard.

"You," I said, which was true. "I'm thinking about you."

"What about me?"

"That—"

"Keeran! Luana!"

I halted. "That's ..."

"Almae," Luana whispered.

We both took off down the side path to the front of the cabin. My mother was running up our porch, hand raised to knock on the door. Didn't the healer say she would sleep until morning?

"Mom? What happened?"

She turned to us, eyes wide. "Thank goodness, you're

here." With disheveled hair and crumpled clothes, she looked like she had just rolled out of bed.

"What happened?" Luana asked, walking to her.

My mother reached a shaking hand to Luana. "It's terrible. Oh my heart, it's horrible."

"What is?" I asked. "What happened?"

"The vision," she muttered, sounding like a crazy woman. "I saw it now. I know what's going to happen."

A scream pierced the night.

"What was that?" I turned toward the bottom of the hill, where it had come from.

Another scream echoed through the air. Then another.

Soon, the screams came all together, nonstop.

"What's happening?" Luana asked, a hint of panic in her voice.

"She's here." A sob came from my mother. "Unity is under attack."

23

My stomach sank.

Isalia was here.

It couldn't be.

What about my plans? We were going to march on her in a few days. We were going to surround the Chateau of the Cursed, and I would challenge her while all of her army was locked inside her manor.

The screams sent a chill up my arms.

Now, she was here, destroying this precious place.

Wyatt and Farrah ran out of their cabin.

"What's happening?" Wyatt asked, coming to our side.

"Isalia is here," Keeran answered, his voice hard.

The screams grew louder and a moment later, people ran up the hill, fleeing whatever was happening at the bottom. In the distance, a thin trail of smoke rose to the air.

"By the moon ..." I turned to Wyatt. "Call the Starlight pack." Wyatt nodded before dashing into the forest. Farrah hesitated. "You stay and help us. We need to rescue Unity's residents."

Almae's stance and expression changed. As if channeling her magic to give her some clarity, the old witch stopped trembling and her gaze focused. "I'll help. Send them up the hill. I'll show them the way to the forest."

With that, Keeran, Farrah, and I ran down the hill, weaving past the supernaturals coming our way.

"Go!" Keeran yelled. "Meet Acalla. Almae! She'll show you the way!"

Farrah stayed halfway up the hill, helping people and knocking on the houses along the streets, waking people up and evacuating them.

As Keeran and I ran toward the bottom of the hill, the crowd became thicker, the screams louder, the smoke closer, the scent of burned wood stronger. We halted near the main street, taking in the damage and expecting surprises. A few people ran past us, but there was no sign of Isalia and her army.

"What's going on?" I asked, glancing around. The people couldn't be screaming for nothing, right? What about the smoke? And Almae's vision ... Isalia was here. I was sure. But where?

"I don't know," Keeran muttered. He was as tense and ready as I was, and when dark figures ran toward us from all sides, he channeled his power. I got ready to shift.

"It's us," Aspen said. He was one of Keeran's warlocks— and the one Keeran trusted the most.

The warlocks halted alongside us, even Finch, the tea-master Keeran had said had refused to join forces with us.

"What's happening?" Boise asked.

"Isalia and her army are here," I said.

"Our priority is helping Unity's residents out," Keeran said, "but be ready to fight."

As if Keeran's words had invoked them, Isalia's army appeared at the end of the street, on the other side of the marketplace. Warlocks and she-wolves advanced toward us, flipping, ripping, and burning the stands. There were still people trapped inside the buildings they were marching by, and they didn't show any mercy. They broke down the doors and attacked them, killing them on sight.

"Oh, no, you don't," I said through gritted teeth.

I ran toward them. Keeran and his warlocks were right behind me.

Mariah, a she-wolf from the time I was Dark Vale's alpha, shifted right before the school's door. The door broke, and she lunged at the people hiding inside. Not used to fighting and using their powers, the supernaturals cowered.

I shifted and went after her. She had her jaw, about to bite someone's arm, when I jumped her. With my increased strength, I threw her against the wall. The wall's paint cracked, and Mariah let out a yelp as she fell to the floor. I didn't give her time to recover. I advanced on her and bit down on her shoulder hard, aiming for an artery. Blood gushed from her wound, and in matter of minutes, she bled out.

Mouth stained, I shifted back and wiped my mouth before turning to the other supernaturals. "Go!" I urged them. "Run. Up the hill. Don't look back."

I escorted them out. Another she-wolf came toward us, but I stopped her before she could get too close. When I looked back, Aspen was protecting them from a warlock. They kept going, until they disappeared up the hill. Hopefully, Farrah would be right there to protect them.

A jolt of energy washed over the main street and the marketplace. I shuddered against it, but it hadn't been intent on harming me. Although our enemies had stopped, alarmed with whatever had hit them.

"That's enough," Keeran said. It was easy to find him. He was standing near a broken stand in the middle of the main street. He looked at the group of warlocks a few feet from him. "Soren is dead. I'm your warlock lord now. Stand down and I'll show you mercy."

One of them spat on the floor. "You're no one."

"So you prefer a deranged werewolf to be your leader. Your alpha?" he asked in a mocking tone, as if the warlocks would be belittled by allowing a wolf to order them around. The shockwave blasted again, and the warlocks shook and grunted against it. The she-wolves weren't doing much better. "As your warlock lord, I order you: stand down!"

To my surprise, a dozen warlocks knelt down on one knee and bowed their heads. I didn't expect Keeran to let them fight alongside us now, not so soon, but at least there were a lot of them out of our way now.

"Ray," I said to the closest warlock. "Lead them—"

A howl made the hairs on my arms stand on end. A she-wolf jumped on one of the surrendering warlocks and ripped him apart in matters of seconds. A moment later, more she-wolves killed all the warlocks who had stood down.

My heart dropped.

No.

With a scream, Keeran let out his magic on the she-wolves. He got one, but the rest dodged his blasts and the fight began anew. I shifted back into a wolf and joined the fray. Still upset about killing that first she-wolf, I tried wounding them so they had to retreat, instead of killing them. But sometimes, it was impossible to defend myself without hurting them for real.

With a hard snap of my teeth, I broke the leg of a she-wolf, so she wouldn't be able to jump. I had just turned to another one, when the marketplace grew quiet.

Realizing what was happening, I shifted into my human form and walked into the street.

On the other end, Isalia strolled into the marketplace, a little baby wrapped in a leather blanket in her arms.

My stomach turned. Did she have to bring her son into this? Was she trying to teach him about being evil and going on killing sprees from birth?

That was despicable.

Her she-wolves lowered their heads at her. Her warlocks stopped fighting, but didn't bow.

On our side, we stopped too, but we held our breaths, waiting for it all to start again.

Isalia halted about ten feet from me. A cruel smile spread through her lips. "Hello there, Luana. Are you ready for our duel?"

I puffed my chest. "Yes."

A she-wolf turned into her human form. Naked and covered in blood, she approached Isalia and took the baby from her.

Isalia's smile widened as she stripped off her clothes. "Any last words?"

"None that you deserve to hear."

Naked, she shifted into a wolf and lunged at me.

24

KEERAN

ISALIA JUMPED FOR LUANA AND MY HEART STOPPED. LUANA turned into her Starlight wolf and got out of the way just in time. Seeing Luana like that for the first time, Isalia hesitated. She was probably surprised Luana had finally returned to her pack.

But her surprise was short-lived, and she rammed into Luana's side with all she had.

My temper rose and a protectiveness tugged in my chest. I was ready to march to them when a hand closed around my arm, stopping me.

"Don't," Romulus said. He and the rest of the Starlight pack had finally arrived in town. "Luana said she wanted to do this herself. You have to let her."

I groaned, remembering my freaking promise to her. Why the hell did I promise that? I jerked my arm free from his grip. "I won't interfere." I turned to him and the rest of the Starlight pack. With them all here, defeating the she-wolves and the other warlocks would be easy. "Let's take the others down," I said, my voice normal, knowing the werewolves could hear me. "Stun without killing, if possible."

The Starlight wolves let out a short howl then lunged toward our enemies. Among them, Wyatt, Farrah, and my warlocks joined the fight.

I wanted to help, but my attention was elsewhere. I couldn't fight knowing Luana was facing Isalia by herself.

The two she-wolves circled each other, sizing up their fangs and claws.

Isalia growled and jumped at Luana.

My gut tightened. Isalia had always been strong and a fast, tricky player. But as the Starlight alpha, Luana was strong and powerful too.

Fast as lightning, Luana got out of Isalia's way. She spun in an arc, and went for Isalia. The two of them met halfway, their paws off the ground, their jaws snapping for their throats. A swipe of Luana's paw hit Isalia right on the muzzle, sending the older she-wolf scurrying back.

Isalia snarled and lunged at Luana again. They tumbled together around the street, knocking down the remainder of broken stands.

Pain exploded in my side, and I screamed in pain and frustration. Another bolt zipped toward me, but before it hit me, I turned toward the warlock attacking me and deflected his strike as if it was smoke in the air.

Freaking warlock, taking my attention from my mate's fight.

I didn't spare a second. I didn't try being diplomatic and talking to him. Instead, I gritted my teeth and sent several little bolts at him. He dodged a few, deflected a couple more, but they were too many and too fast for him. The bolts struck him in the chest, shoulders, and legs. The warlock felt on his knees, his body numb with my spell.

He blinked at me, before face-planting on the ground.

I would deal with him later.

Feeling anxious, I turned back to Luana's fight. With her super speed and strength, Luana rammed Isalia in the side. The evil she-wolf fell. Luana opened her mouth wide, ready to strike, but Isalia swiped her paw on the ground, sending a pile of dust and soot to Luana's face.

Shaking her head, Luana stepped back.

And Isalia attacked. With a great leap, she pressed her paws on Luana's side, pushing her down. Then, a blade appeared in Isalia's mouth. What the hell?

"Hey!" I called. "That's cheating!"

If she could cheat, I could too, right? Because promise or not, I couldn't let Isalia hurt Luana like that. Any kind of weapon was forbidden during a werewolf duel, and it was clear Isalia wasn't interested in playing fair, as usual.

I was about to charge in the fight when Isalia dropped the blade and stepped back. She shifted into her human body, and eyes wide, she stared at something right behind me. I turned and found the door to the infirmary broken and Soren standing under the doorframe.

Someone had broken in, probably to kill whoever was hiding in there, but upon seeing Soren in there, they let him out.

"Soren," she whispered. Like magic, the dagger disappeared from her hand. What the hell was that? "My love, Soren." Naked, she ran past Luana, past me, and rushed to my father. "Oh, Soren, you're alive!" Isalia held on to his arms, but in his zombie-like state, Soren didn't even look at her. She shook him. "What's wrong?" she asked, trying to catch his eyes. She glanced at me, her gaze desperate. "What's wrong with him?"

"He's no more," my mother said, walking into the marketplace. Despite her messy hair and clothes, she looked composed. Much better than when she was losing it to the prophecies. "His magic is gone, along with himself. Now, he's just a shell."

Isalia's gaze turned from despair to rage. "Who did this?" She fixed her hateful stare at me. "You. You did this, didn't you?" She let go of my father and turned to me. "You killed him! You know that, right? Like this, Soren is dead."

"I—" I closed my mouth. I didn't owe her any explanations. Moreover, I didn't have any affection for that horrible man. He got what he deserved, plain and simple.

"I'll kill you!" Isalia came at me. She turned in mid-jump, surprising me.

I lifted my arms, ready to blast her with my magic.

Luana pounced on Isalia. They landed on the ground a few feet from me. Isalia was down on her side, her neck stained red, her eyes open and glazed. Luana stood over her, her mouth dripping with blood.

Luana had done it. She had killed Isalia. She won.

In shock, Luana shifted back into her human form and stepped back from Isalia's body. She wiped at her mouth, as if disgusted with what she had done.

Around us, the fight died out too. The she-wolves were too wounded to keep fighting, and if they tried anything, Luana could order them to stand down now. The warlocks had surrendered.

Slowly, I approached Luana. "It had to be done."

"I know," she muttered. She turned to me. "It doesn't mean I enjoyed it."

"I know." I took her hand in mine. "That's what makes you so special, you know. Because you would rather find a solution other than violence. Now you can. Now, we'll rule and set an example. No more fights. No more wars. No more killings."

Luana stepped into me and rested her head against my chest. "That's all I want."

I ran a hand down her back. "I know." I frowned, remembering something. "She had a blade in her hand. It appeared and disappeared like magic."

Luana nodded. "We communicated during the fight. I asked her if she was going to cheat using the blade again, and she explained she got it from a witch long ago. It can be imbued with several kinds of poison, and she was proud of how she could summon it out of nowhere."

I nodded, finally making sense of that damn weapon.

Flanked by Wyatt and Farrah, a she-wolf approached us. She was carrying Isalia's baby.

My brother.

"What do I with it?" she asked, her voice disgusted. "I don't want it."

I swallowed hard. This was my brother. In some way, he was my responsibility, especially since Luana and I had taken down his parents. But I wasn't ready. I wasn't ready to have a kid of my own, much less one I wasn't sure how to feel about.

"If I may," a Starlight wolf said. She walked up to us, keeping her head low. "My alpha, I recently lost my pup during birth." Her lower lip trembled. "He was too weak and didn't resist." She raised her gaze to Luana. "If you allow me, I'll take this pup and raised him as if he were mine."

Luana looked at me. "What do you think?" I couldn't

think of any other solution. I nodded. Luana offered a soft smile to the wolf. "You may have him."

With a huge smile, the wolf grabbed the baby and cradled him in her arms. "Thank you." She bowed to Luana, to me. "Thank you so much." She stepped back, falling in line with the rest of her pack.

Trying my best to push my brother out of my mind, I glanced around. The main street and the marketplace were destroyed, there were bodies and blood everywhere, the scent of smoke and death hung in the air, and we had plenty of she-wolves and repentant warlocks to deal with.

I let out a long breath. "We might have won the war, but it seems we still have a lot of work to do."

My mother stepped to our side. "The sooner we start cleaning up and dealing with our prisoners, the faster we'll be done."

"She's right, you know," Luana said.

My mother tsked. "Don't you know? Mothers are always right."

I rolled my eyes. "All right. Less chatting. More working."

Like a team, like a tight family, we started repairs to Unity.

25

I LOOKED OUT THE WINDOW, AMAZED AT ALL WE HAD BEEN ABLE to do in only six months. Since defeating Isalia and cleaning up the mess in Unity, Keeran and I decided we didn't belong there.

We belonged in a place of our own, a place where we could be Starlight pack alpha and warlock lord together. Because of that, we started rebuilding Starlight Vale. There was still a lot of work to do, but the palace was mostly done, along with most of the town. The houses in town were now the home of the Starlight wolves and warlocks—two races united as one, living together as peers and friends.

Since our move two weeks ago, Almae had come to visit us once. She even had her own quarters in the palace, but despite Keeran's arguments, she insisted on returning to Unity.

"They need me there," she kept saying.

I believed her. She had founded that paradise. After a long, long life, she would someday die there too.

But today, she was here. She had arrived yesterday, actually, to spend some time with us before the celebration tonight.

"Here," Romulus said, handing me another piece of paper.

It was hard tearing my gaze from the beautiful town below—the gray stone, the brown tree branches, the green leaves, and the sun setting behind the valley, giving everything a warm, golden shine.

We had moved here two weeks ago, but no other place had felt like home before, not like this place did.

"What is this?" I asked, finally glancing at the paper.

"The menu for tonight's celebration," he said. "We added the changes you requested."

I read over the menu. Roasted pork, au gratin potatoes, plenty of blood for the vampires, a raw lamb on a platter for the werewolves. To please all races, there were over twenty-fives items on the menu. Hopefully, no one would complain that the Starlight Vale hosts weren't considerate.

"And the wine?" I asked, returning the menu to Romulus.

"Already chilled and ready to go." He took the paper from me. "Any more changes, my alpha?"

"Even if I had any, I don't think we would have time for that now, would we?"

"You're right." He bowed his head to me. "I'll go check on the kitchen now then."

I nodded once. "Thank you."

Romulus left the large office. I watched him for a moment, but soon my gaze found the crystal rose on top of my oak desk, where it now rested in a simple glass vase. According to Keeran, the magic was still active, but I hadn't needed to use it in the last six months. I liked having it near me, though. I liked looking at it and remembering Keeran's love when he made it for me.

Then, my eyes shifted to the second desk in the room: Keeran's. He was seated there, lost in thought while reading a thick leather book, with Aspen right over his shoulder. Since Isalia's defeat, Aspen had become Keeran's right hand, and Boise had become his left one.

I smiled, completely smitten and happy about our life. Here my mate was, occupying the office which had once been my father's with me, ruling over our kingdom of sorts, sharing our every moment, loving each other unconditionally.

It was the perfect life.

There was only one thing missing.

Two actually.

Wyatt and Farrah.

They had been here while we cleaned up Unity, had helped the wounded, had buried the dead, and had made sure everyone and everything were okay. But once the dust settled, once we started talking about moving to the Starlight Vale and everything that we would need to make a quick renovation of the town, they had disappeared.

Wyatt left first. Without saying goodbye. He didn't even leave a note behind. After all we had been through, it hurt. But I knew why he did it. Because if he had told me he was leaving, if he had said goodbye, I wouldn't have let him leave. By the moon, he was only seventeen! A lone teenage wolf in a dangerous supernatural world? I didn't like it. I sent some of the best scouts from my pack after him, but they couldn't find a trace of him. My stomach twisted every time I thought about him, about what could have happened to him, if he was okay, or if his depression had come back, and he was lying in a dark alley wasting away. But other than fret and worry, send out scouts to find him, or ask Keeran to cast a tracking spell—which never worked—what else could I do?

Then, there was Farrah. A day after Wyatt left, she approached Keeran and me and said goodbye to us. I tried convincing her to stay, to help me find Wyatt, but she was adamant on leaving.

"I'm going to hide from Prince Lark," she had said. "Hopefully, he'll never find me."

I hoped so too. It was my fault she was now engaged to that evil fae prince. I offered anything I could do to help her, to change her fate, but she said that the fae prince wouldn't stop now, no matter what we did or offered or begged to let this go.

So, she left to hide from her impending wedding.

Speaking of weddings, Keeran and I hadn't officially married, not like Drake and Thea had. We were mates for life. We didn't need huge ceremonies to prove that.

"Here," Keeran said, closing the leather book and handing it to Aspen. "Thank you."

"Yes, my lord." Aspen took the book and left the room, closing the door behind him.

Keeran stared at me, a half smile on his lips. "You look absolutely stunning."

I rolled my eyes. He had said that an hour ago, when I finished getting ready for the party tonight. One of the masterful designers from the Starlight pack had made me a dark green gown with dark brown accents. The bodice was a low-cut corset style, which exposed a little cleavage. The fabric bunched up over the shoulders, but opened up in the back, revealing a lot of my skin. The skirt was long, with a slit over my left leg, and a small train in the back. Tiny emerald green beads covered the fabric, giving it a shimmering glow every time I moved.

"You don't look too bad either," I said.

As if wanting to show off, Keeran stood from his chair and buttoned the jacket of his tuxedo. He wore a dark green shirt and tie, which matched my dress.

With his eyes on mine, he stalked to me. "That's a lot of skin showing. I'm not sure I can let you go like that."

I snorted. "As if you have a choice."

He grabbed my wrists and pulled me to him. "I meant," he whispered in my ear, "letting you go before I tasted you." My breath hitched; my body warmed. Keeran wrapped one arm around me, splaying his fingers on my bare back. "I want you. I always want you."

He leaned into me.

I was ready. I was ready to mess up my pretty dress and hair and makeup, and have rough, hard sex with him right in our office, on the evening of our grand celebration while our people waited.

A knock reverberated on the door before his lips even touched mine.

It was like a bucket of cold water that extinguished my desire and spiked my temper.

"Yes," I said through gritted teeth.

Chuckling, Keeran took half a step back. A moment later, the door opened and Meira stuck her head inside. "My alpha. Lord Drake, Queen Thea, and Princess Aurora are here."

"Let them in," Keeran said, with a smile.

Meira stepped aside and the gorgeous trio paraded inside our office.

Aurora took two composed steps before she started running and launched herself into Keeran's arms. He caught her easily, and pulled her up against him. My heart fluttered a little, seeing how great he was with children.

Aurora turned her bright gray gaze to me. "I'm mad at you."

I forced a gasp. "Me? Why?"

"Because you don't visit often enough."

I smiled. "Oh, my princess, I've been very, very busy." I took her hand in mine. "But I promise you, I'll visit more often. Does that sound good?"

She nodded, making her long black curls bounce. With her satin pink gown and a diamond tiara on top of her head, Aurora looked more like a giant, fluffy cupcake than a little girl.

She hooked her arm around my neck and pulled me into a three-hug. I laughed.

"I heard that," Drake said.

Aurora turned in my arms, and I looked at them. Drake looked every bit like a vampire lord in a black tuxedo and burgundy tie, and beside him, Thea was just gorgeous. She wore a tight red dress, and her blond hair was pulled up in a complicated bun, red rubies adorning the knots. A few precisely curled strands fell down her neck and the side of her head, framing her beautiful face.

"What did you hear?" I asked.

"That you'll visit more often," Drake said. "We'll be counting on that."

Thea nodded. "We certainly will."

"How was the trip?" Keeran asked. He passed all of Aurora's weight to me and went to the bar behind his desk.

"What trip?" Drake joked. "DuMoir Castle is a little over a day from here. That's nothing."

Thea shuddered. "I don't recommend traveling with an overly agitated half-witch, half-vampire toddler, though."

Aurora rolled her eyes. "Mommy, I can hear you."

"Now that!" Thea pointed to her daughter. "She's not even two years old yet, and she's already talking like a teenager. I'm not sure I can handle years of that."

We all chuckled.

Keeran came back with a glass full of blood for Drake and wine for Thea. "You're just saying that. She's the cutest thing ever."

Drake stared at the little princess in my arms. "That is true." He then turned his gaze to Keeran and me. "Before we start the party and celebrate the comeback of Starlight Vale, I just want to say congratulations."

I frowned. "On?"

"Succeeding," he said.

Thea exchanged a glance with him. "There was a moment a few months ago, when we thought you two wouldn't be able to handle Soren and Isalia by yourselves. We were ready to send in some help out."

"But as it turned out, you two surprised us and proved you're capable," Drake added. He raised his glass high. "To Luana and Keeran, a prosperous union and a peaceful Starlight Vale."

We cheered with him.

Then, another knock came from the door. This time, Meira didn't wait for a reply, she opened the door and said, "The guests are arriving, my alpha. You should move on to the ballroom."

"Right," I said. "Thank you." After a bow, she left. I smiled at Thea and Drake. "Let's go to the ballroom."

"Sure," Thea said.

I put Aurora down, but took her hand in mine. She took Keeran's hand, too, and the three of us walked out of the office with linked hands.

Keeran smiled at me from over Aurora's head. "She's just precious."

"Are you thinking about kids, Keeran?" I whispered.

"Later," he whispered back. "I'll definitely want to have kids with you, Luana, but later. First I want to enjoy you." He winked.

"I can hear you, you know," Aurora said.

I gasped. Keeran barked out a laugh. Even Drake, who was a few steps in front of us, swallowed a chuckle.

My cheeks flamed and I tried recomposing myself before we reached the ballroom. Thankfully, we stopped a few steps later, when we bumped into Elisa and Prince Cain. Elisa was Thea's second at the Silverblood Estate, and Prince Cain was the closest prince to Drake after the battle at DuMoir Castle almost two years ago.

"Good evening," Elisa said with a small smile. She was a pretty witch with long copper hair and bright green eyes. Tonight, she wore a black gown with a simple, straight cut, except that the fabric changed colors when she moved—purple, dark blue, dark green. It was mesmerizing.

"Good to see you again," Prince Cain said. He was as tall as Drake, and had short brown hair and hazel eyes. He wore a fancy black tuxedo with a black tie. Very elegant.

Together, the seven of us walked the rest of the way to ballroom.

Keeran and I were ushering our friends in when Boise approached us.

"My lord," he said, bowing his head to Keeran. "I just

received an important report." He offered the folded paper to Keeran.

Keeran shook his head. "Leave it on my desk. I'll read it tomorrow."

"My lord, I think it's important. You might not want to do anything about it tonight, but you should read it."

With a frown, Keeran took the folded paper from Boise and read it. I leaned beside him and read it too.

Increase fae activity close to the Starlight Vale territory. None of them seem friendly.

Keeran stared at me. "It couldn't be Farrah and Daleigh, could it?"

I shrugged. "I don't know." I glanced at the report again. "We have no idea where Farrah went. She could be far from Daleigh." Or she could be hiding with her brother, hoping he would protect her from the fae prince.

"Just ... increase the number of patrols around the town for tonight," Keeran said to Boise. "Don't do anything rash. If you see anything suspicious, come and find me."

"Yes, my lord." Boise tipped his head and marched out.

"What now?" I asked, a little worried. All we needed was an army of fae warriors attacking our town, destroying our palace, and terrorizing our people and our guests.

Keeran frowned. "I wonder if it's Prince Lark, searching for Farrah."

It was a possibility. Prince Lark had seemed like a wicked emperor in that fortress of his. "Should we cancel and send everyone away?" I asked.

Keeran shook his head. "No, not tonight. I bet this is nothing. By tomorrow, they'll have moved on and we'll be safe." He slipped his hand in mine. "Tonight, let's forget about wars and battles and blood. Tonight, let's celebrate all our accomplishments and our return to Starlight Vale."

He was right. There was no reason to worry about this report, not yet. For all we knew, it could simply be some fae marching through the forest nearby, going somewhere else.

I smiled at my mate. "Sounds heavenly."

Holding tight to his hand, I let him guide me into the ballroom, where we danced the night away with our friends, and I wished life could always be this wonderful.

With Keeran, I knew it would be.

THANK YOU

Thank you for reading *The Crystal Rose*!

Reviews are very important for authors. If you liked my book, please consider leaving a review on your favorite vendor and/or on goodreads, please!

Did you like this book? You can check out other books of mine, both FREE:

Heart Seeker (The Fire Heart Chronicles book 1): an urban fantasy series about a young woman who finds herself at the center of a mysterious supernatural world.

Destiny Gift (The Everlast Series book 1): a post-apocalyptic urban fantasy series about a young woman with a special power that can save the world.

Find more about my books here: www.julianahaygert.com/books/

. . .

Don't forget to sign up for my Newsletter to find out about new releases, cover reveals, giveaways, and more!

If you want to see exclusive teasers, help me decide on covers, read excerpts, talk about books, etc, join my reader group on Facebook: Juliana's Club!

I have an exclusive novella set in the Rite World that is just for my newsletter subscribers!

Click here to sign-up and receive your book!

THE VAMPIRE HUNT
A Rite World Novella

Norah is a demon hunter, one of the best graduated from the Blackthorn Hunters Academy. When she's sent to investigate a case concerning demons in a small town, she runs into a very arrogant vampire. Her first instinct is to kill him, after all, he's a supernatural and demon hunters are taught to end all evil.

Cain is a vampire prince. Because of his status, he's in charge of making sure humans don't find out about his kind. During a routine investigation, he bumps into a very sexy demon hunter and he wonders what she's doing on his way.

However, the case grows much bigger for Norah and Cain to handle alone. To find the truth and win this battle, the vampire and the demon hunter will have to hunt together—without killing each other.

How well could this end?

ABOUT THE AUTHOR

While USA Today Bestselling Author Juliana Haygert dreams of being Wonder Woman, Buffy, or a blood elf shadow priest, she settles for the less exciting—but equally gratifying—life as a wife, a mother, and an author. She resides in North Carolina and spends her days writing about kick-ass heroines and the heroes who drive them crazy.

Subscribe to her mailing list to receive emails of announcement, events, and other fun stuff related to her writing and her books: www.bit.ly/JuHNL

For more information:
www.julianahaygert.com

facebook.com/julianahaygert

twitter.com/juliana_haygert

instagram.com/juliana.haygert

goodreads.com/juliana_haygert

pinterest.com/julianahaygert

bookbub.com/authors/juliana-haygert

ALSO BY JULIANA HAYGERT

To find links and more info, go to:

www.julianahaygert.com/books/

Shorts

Into the Darkest Fire

Tested

Rite World: Blackthorn Hunters Academy

The Demon Kiss (Book 1)

The Hunter Secret (Book 2)

The Soul Bond (Book 3)

The Shadow Trials (Book 4)

The Infernal Curse (Book 5)

Rite World

The Vampire Heir (Book 1)

The Witch Queen (Book 2)

The Immortal Vow (Book 3)

The Warlock Lord (Book 4)

The Wolf Consort (Book 5)

The Crystal Rose (Book 6)

The Wolf Forsaken (Book 7)

The Fae Bound (Book 8)

The Blood Pact (Book 9)

The Wyth Courts

Winter King (Book 1)

Spring Warrior (Book 2)

Summer Prince (Book 3)

Autumn Rebel (Book 4)

The Fire Heart Chronicles

Heart Seeker (Book 1)

Flame Caster (Book 2)

Sorrow Bringer (Book 3)

Earth Shaker (Novella)

Soul Wanderer (Book 4)

Fate Summoner (Book 5)

War Maiden (Book 6)

The Everlast Series

Destiny Gift (Book 1)

Soul Oath (Book 2)

Cup of Life (Book 3)

Everlasting Circle (Book 4)

Willow Harbor Series

Hunter's Revenge (Book 3)

Siren's Song (Book 5)

Breaking Series

Breaking Free (Book 1)

Breaking Away (Book 2)

Breaking Through (Book 3)

Breaking Down (Book 4)

Standalones

Daughter of Darkness